P.S., IT'S MURDER

The moment Alice had gone Lady Heron began to fumble at the tiny velvet bag that still hung round her wrist.

"Quick," she said. "The key's in here. Get it out for me."

John extracted a small key.

"The wardrobe," she said. "The bottom shelf. The black workbox. Take it out."

"Is this it?" asked John, lifting up the black box. Memories of death-bed scenes from famous Victorian novels came into his mind and filled it with the wildest ideas. Was this her will? Was he to witness it? Or destroy it? Had she left him money because he had made friends with her cat?

"The letters," gasped Lady Heron. "Take them away. Stuff them in your pockets. All of them. Hurry up, hurry, hurry, hurry."

"What am I to do with them?" he asked in a whisper.

"Keep them in a safe place," she replied. "But don't read them. Only if I should die," she went on, lowering her eyes. "If you hear of my death you are to read them and take action."

ANNA CLARKE

THE DEATHLESS AND THE DEAD

CHARTER BOOKS, NEW YORK

This Charter book contains the complete
text of the original hardcover edition.
It has been completely reset in a typeface
designed for easy reading, and was printed
from new film.

THE DEATHLESS AND THE DEAD

A Charter Book / pulished by arrangement with
William Collins Sons & Co.

PRINTING HISTORY
Collins edition published 1976
Charter edition / August 1989

ISBN: 1-55773-230-2

Charter Books are published by The Berkley Publishing Group,
200 Madison Avenue, New York, New York 10016.
The name "CHARTER" and the "C" logo
are trademarks belonging to Charter Communications, Inc.

PRINTED IN THE UNITED STATES OF AMERICA

10 9 8 7 6 5 4 3 2 1

1

"It must have been somewhere about here," said John, pulling the elderly Morris Minor on to the grass verge of the southern Oxford bypass, "that she died."

"All of sixty years ago," said his companion with such gentle irony that he failed to notice it. "Are you hoping to find some evidence?" she went on. "A lock of her raven hair caught in a hawthorn bush? A scrap of paper nailed to a gate containing one priceless line of Emily Witherington's deathless verse?"

The mockery was now too obvious to be ignored.

"Of course not," said John a little testily. "There's no question about how she died. Her bike ran out of control as she came down Boar's Hill and she fell off and broke her neck. It's all in the reports of the inquest. The police seem to have been very thorough. Of course it would be quite ridiculous to try doing any Sherlock Holmes stuff after all these years."

"Not to mention the fact that in the late eighteen-nineties

there was no bypass road and the whole landscape must have looked completely different from what it does now."

The girl laid particular stress on the word "now," perhaps with the aim of dragging John's mind away from the past and back into their own world of the early nineteen-sixties.

"Yes, it would have been quite different," he agreed rather unhappily. He put an arm round her shoulders and they sat silent for a few minutes, staring out at a horrible disorder of bulldozers and mud and brutally gashed sections of hillside. The mist of the late February afternoon blotted out the distant view of the lovely city. There was nothing within their range of vision save this no-man's-land of roadworks.

The girl shivered a little. She was wearing a fur hat and an expensive tweed coat, but the air even inside the car was very chill.

"I'm sorry, Alice," said John, withdrawing his arm and starting the car with rather a jerk. "I shouldn't have brought you up here. Only it seemed such a good chance when Mrs. Willey offered to lend me the car for the afternoon."

"It was very kind of her," said the girl formally. "She's a most unusual landlady."

They drove a little way in silence, ill at ease with each other. A shadow had come between them; the ghost of the poet Emily, the subject of John's researches and the reason for his being in Oxford at all. Beautiful, passionate Emily, who had written love poetry that had shocked the more timid spirits of her own times, but that could still move the reader's heart and impress the critics enough to gain her a place in a series of studies of minor Victorian poets. She had her own tiny place among the immortals. It might have been a much bigger place if fate had not decreed otherwise. She might well have stood high up on the roll of honour, challenging the greatest names throughout the centuries if her gifts had had the chance to come to maturity. But she had been impulsive and wild, courting danger and careless of her own well-being, and one of those rash excursions of hers had led to the cutting short of all that bright promise at the tragically early age of twenty.

"I thought," said John as they waited in a long queue of traffic that was trying to negotiate a half-finished round-about, "that I might get some sort of feeling about how she felt on the day she died if I came to have a look at the place. I've got a sort of idea that she might deliberately have ridden to her death. It's just a feeling. There's no evidence for it. But I ought to have had the sense to know it would be hopeless."

There was hurt pride as well as disappointment in his voice. The fair girl in the expensive clothes glanced at his handsome sulky profile. He was terribly touchy and he could not stand being teased, this clever boy from the back streets of Leeds who had won his way into one of the foremost universities in the country, and who so incongru-ously had a passion for Victorian art and literature and in particular for the work of the poet in question. He was a dreadful bore on the subject of his poet, but apart from that he was not a bore at all, rather exciting in fact, quite different from her cousin Lionel who was in the Guards, and indeed from any other young man she had ever met in her rather too sheltered life. She was conscious of two equally strong, but apparently quite separate impulses: a perfectly ridiculous jealousy of the poet Emily, who had been dead for sixty years, and a longing to put her arms round John's tense and angry body and comfort him as if he had been a disappointed small boy.

She was very inexperienced and immature, for all her air of sophistication, and she did not yet realize that this combination of symptoms added up to a diagnosis that she was well on the way to being deeply in love.

"You'll find plenty of other ways to get the feel of Emily and her work," she said soothingly. "In fact I might be able to help you myself."

"You might?" He turned towards her just before the traffic moved on. His face was eager and alive again.

She swallowed the little lump of regret that the eagerness was not directed solely towards herself, and said quietly: "I think my uncle met her once or twice when he was a young man—my Great-Uncle Roderick, I mean, who brought me up."

This remark had such an electrifying effect upon John that he narrowly escaped running into the car in front.

"Good God!" he exclaimed when they were moving steadily forward again. "What a stroke of luck. That's absolutely super, Alice. Why ever didn't you tell me before? When can I come and meet your uncle?"

She did not answer for some time and when at last she spoke her words were disappointing to him.

"I think I had better tell him first about you and your research and see how he reacts. It's rather a bad time to be asking favours because he's very angry with me for leaving home and going to live in Meg's flat. But after all, I'm twenty-one and it's time I had some sort of a life of my own."

"Of course," agreed John automatically. Alice's little bid for independence was at this moment of far less interest to him than her uncle's acquaintance with Emily Witherington.

"What a stroke of luck," he repeated presently. "I'll be able to tell Professor Woodward's seminar that I've actually had an interview with an eye-witness. They'll be green with envy. We'll be meeting again on Wednesday week. I suppose there's no chance of my coming to talk to your uncle about Emily before next week-end?"

"John, I think I ought to explain that it won't be easy," began Alice, and then stopped. They were being overtaken by a noisy lorry that precluded all speech.

"Sorry," said John when it had passed. "What did you say?"

"I said I'll do my best to persuade Uncle Rod to tell you everything he can remember," she said.

"That's my girl," he said, beaming at her as they drew up at a terrace of red-brick houses in one of the more modest streets of north Oxford. "There's crumpets for tea and Mrs. Willey's made me a cake."

"She spoils you," said Alice as she followed him down the area steps to his two rooms in the basement.

"Why not? I do a lot for her, and after all, I'm a poor motherless boy."

He grinned cheerfully, but Alice was not deceived. She had heard all about how John's mother, after flitting from one man to another, had finally flown away for ever, leaving the ten-year-old boy and his father to console each other. A lot of John's touchiness and cockiness, she decided, could be attributed to this old pain.

"When you meet Auntie Belle and Uncle Rod," she said later as they sat toasting crumpets in front of the dilapidated gas-fire, "would you mind very much not letting them know that your parents are divorced?"

"Why, are they Roman Catholics?"

"No, but it might prejudice them against you."

John flushed and averted his face. "If you're regretting your offer," he said, "if you're ashamed of me and would rather I didn't meet them—"

"No, no, no," she cried vehemently. "It's not that."

"What is it, then?"

"I'm afraid they might hurt you," she said, letting her head droop so low that her fair hair fell over her face.

"Hurt me?" he echoed incredulously. "How on earth can they hurt me? Don't you think I'm capable of taking care of myself?"

"In any normal circumstances, yes. But Uncle Rod and Auntie Belle aren't normal. I don't mean they are mad or anything, and I love them very much because they are all I've got in the world. But I'm not blind to their faults and I can see the effect they have on other people. It's terrifying."

"Terrifying!" He laughed. "An old man and an old woman."

"Yes, terrifying," she repeated very soberly. "They hate each other, you know. I've always realized that, ever since I was a little girl. They tear each other to pieces the whole time, whether there is anyone else present or not. I sometimes wonder why it is that one of them hasn't murdered the other long ago. I suppose it's because they enjoy quarreling so much that they'd miss it if one of them was dead."

She looked at John ruefully. "You see, my dear, you're not the only one with an unhappy home background."

"Poor little Alice." He pulled her towards him. "Poor little orphan Alice. You seem to be even worse off than I am. At least Dad and I get on well with each other. Poor little rich girl."

She winced. "Please don't say that, John."

"But it's true, isn't it, love?" He played with her fingers, holding them up one by one, and lingering longest over the one that bore a ring with red stones that sparkled in the light from the old standard lamp.

"Yes," she said miserably. "I have a big allowance and I shall inherit a lot more when Uncle dies. Every bit of it if I marry my cousin Lionel which I've no intention of doing. He's a fool and a bore."

"And isn't John Broome just a bit of a bore too? Come on, confess. Confess that you don't share my passion for a certain Victorian lady poet?"

"I've offered to help you," she said in a muffled voice.

"You have and I appreciate it and I'd like to hold you to the offer. But first of all we've got to get one thing quite clear. I'm not after your money, Alice."

"I know you're not."

She released herself and they stared at each other.

"Though I'm not sure that it wouldn't make it easier if you were," she said at last. "At least in that case you would have to pretend that you cared for me."

He flared up. "I hate pretending."

"I know you do, and you're going to have to do a hell of a lot of it if you're to get anything at all out of Uncle Rod. Your blunt Yorkshire honesty isn't going to serve you there, my lad. Subtlety is the word. And self-control. And patience. And respectful submission. And all sorts of disagreeable things like that."

"I can be all that if I have to," said John rather sulkily.

"And if it leads you to your Emily. You'd go through fire for her sweet sake." Alice leapt to her feet, held a hand to her forehead, and proclaimed in a melodramatic manner: "What have you done, Alice Heron, that you should suffer such contempt? That you should be used as a mere instrument, a signpost in the pursuit of a literary lady, and a dead one at that!"

But John did not laugh. "I'm sorry," he said. "It's beastly selfish of me. I can see that now. I'd better give it up. Asking your uncle about Emily, I mean. It's obviously going to make it awkward for you if I meet your folks and it'll completely ruin our own relationship, which would be a pity, because I thought we were getting on rather well, weren't we, Alice?"

"Oh, John!"

He could see the tears in her eyes and hear them in her voice as he went on, conscious of his own self-sacrificing virtue, but also conscious of a great upswell of more disturbing emotions, of pity, of tenderness, of a great desire to comfort and protect. And behind these again there was fear, an awful hollow fear of having these tender feelings of his shriveled up by mockery.

"It's always a big hurdle to get over, meeting other people's families," he said, "even if they come from the same class of society. But it's far worse when there's a difference like that between you and me, with a sheet-metal worker on one side and a Colonial Governor on the other. Your uncle was a very big shot, wasn't he?"

She nodded unhappily.

"And a Governor-General and Baronet of Ancient Lineage on the other," repeated John with great emphasis. "Well, I don't drink my tea out of my saucer and I believe that my old man's as good as he is, any day, and I've worked for every bit of education and every chance I've ever had and I'm not ashamed of it, and I know you aren't either, but it's not what we feel, it's what they feel, and it will be absolute hell for you to sit there knowing they are despising me, so I think the best thing is for us to forget all about it and I'm sorry I pestered you. I ought to have had more sense."

"Oh, John," was all she said, but her whole heart was in the words.

"Then that's that," he said briskly. "Now what shall we do this evening? Shall we go to a film?"

"Yes, let's," she cried, but as he stepped forward to kiss her she pushed him away, frowning, and said: "Just a minute. I want to think. I want to do what's best for us both. Really best in the long run, I mean. Not just the easiest way out of a present difficulty. If you feel I've let you down over Emily Witherington aren't you going to feel resentful and start going off me?"

"Oh, to hell with Emily Witherington!" cried John, a remark that he had never imagined it possible for him to make, but at that moment it happened to be perfectly sincere.

"Shush. Don't blaspheme," she said, smiling now but still holding him at arm's length. "I'm quite serious about this. I really do want to work out what's best for our relationship."

"All right," he said resignedly. "Let's weigh the pros and cons. Though really, of all the cold-blooded ways of dealing with the delicate matter of human feelings— "

"Shush," she said again. "I'm not cold-blooded. Now listen."

He did listen, and then she listened while he spoke.

They talked for some time, diligently analysing their own emotions and reactions, and incidentally falling more and more deeply in love. They did not know that they were holding much more than their own fate in the balance; that the decision they would eventually reach after the conscientious adjustment of the scales was one that could closely affect other lives than their own and that might even result in the complete rewriting of one small section in the great volume that contained the history of English literature.

They were of one mind now, at ease with each other, but there was still a third presence. It was the ghost of the poet Emily.

— 2 —

A couple of weeks later, when the first crocuses were appearing in the North Oxford gardens, and behind the chill March winds one could feel the first little breath of spring, John and Alice walked hand in hand along a quiet cul-de-sac in the neighbourhood of the University Parks.

"You must admire the cat," said Alice, "because he practically rules the household, and you must stand up for yourself as much as you can with Auntie, but be very deferential to Uncle Rod and just keep silent if you're in any doubt about what to say."

"Anything else?" asked John.

"Yes. There's Letty. Letty Mann, the companion-help."

"Oh, the servants," said John, putting on what he imagined to be an upper-class voice. He was terribly nervous, and this was his way of trying to hide it.

"There's only two of them," said Alice. "You probably won't see Jimmy. He's worked for Uncle for years, and he looks after the garden and the car. The cleaning woman only comes in the mornings and Letty does the rest. You'll find her embarrassing. You can't help feeling sorry for her but at the same time she irritates you. She's one of nature's victims, but spiteful with it. I dread to think what's going on in her mind while she's bowing and scraping. I should think she hates us all like poison. But she's stuck it out for three years now, which is a record. Most of the resident helps have a nervous breakdown after six months."

"Alice." John gripped her hand more tightly and pulled her to a halt. They stood a few yards away from the front gate of the ugliest of all the huge yellow-brick Victorian villas that stood in Blenheim Close. "Alice, are you trying to tell me that you'd rather not go after all? Shall we call it off? It's not too late. I'll turn back and you can make some excuse for my not coming."

Her grey eyes looked up at him pleadingly from under the little fur cap.

"I'm such a coward," she whispered. "I really am afraid. If you knew how I loathe rows and what an effort it is to me to stand up to Uncle, because I really do love him too. Help me not to be such a coward. Help me, John."

His hands were bare, and he could feel the softness of the leather of her gloves as she clutched him.

"I want to help you," he said. "Now and always if you'll let me. But this is something you must decide for yourself. I'll turn back if you say so, Alice, and I'll do my very best not to let it make any difference to you and me."

"But it will," she said. "There'll always be the ghost of Emily between us."

He said nothing. Their own future, and the fate of several other people, and a little corner of the great book of English poetry once more trembled in the balance.

"I can feel her now," went on Alice. "She's haunting us.

She's got a grip on you and she'll haunt us for ever if we don't let her have her way."

"Darling." He smiled at her and gripped her hands tightly. "Who's being fanciful now? I thought I was supposed to be the one who always let my imagination run away with me."

"Can't you feel her? Can't you hear her saying, 'Go on, go on, ask your uncle, ask your aunt, ask anyone who ever knew me.' Can't you hear her, John?"

"Of course I can. That's why I'm writing this book about her. She's my mystery lady."

"And she's also your whole career. You'll make your name with this book. The critics will rave over it and you'll be a Professor of English Literature before you're thirty and you'll be invited to lecture in America and the world will recognize you as the authority and you'll look down your nose at stupid ignorant people like me."

"Aren't you rather running ahead a little?" said John, laughing. "Though it certainly would be a tremendous boost if I made a success of this book, and if I can get some first-hand information from someone who actually knew her it could make a lot of difference to the final result."

He had not meant to tip the scales again like this, but she had as good as forced him into it.

"Come on," she said, tugging at his hand. "What are we waiting for? They have afternoon tea at half past four precisely and woe betide anyone who is late."

Alice had kept her key to the house, since she still spent a lot of her time there, and as she pushed open the front door John had an impression of a dark and gloomy hall, lit only by the light coming from an open door at the far end. Emerging from this door was an enormous trolley laden with silver and crockery, and pushing it was a short dark woman clad in an overall of such violently discordant colours that they quite blotted out any impression of its wearer.

Alice gave a barely audible sigh. "It's all right. We're not late," she said. "You can leave your coat and scarf here."

She indicated a tall round hat-stand at the foot of the stairs, and then moved forward to help the other woman negotiate an awkward corner with the trolley.

"This is Miss Mann, John," she said. "Mainstay of the Heron household. Letty, meet my friend John Broome."

"Hullo," said John feebly, looking down into a face that was younger and more prepossessing than he had at first thought, and whose eyes held an expression both wary and inquisitive. His hands hung clumsily at his sides; Miss Mann's were still gripping the tea-trolley. Was it socially correct for him, in his present capacity as guest of the family, to offer to shake hands with the paid domestic help? Uneasily he realized that this was probably only the first of many such pitfalls. The way to the wonderful goal of a talk with the man who had actually known Emily was no doubt strewn with them. Alice came to his rescue.

"Would you go on in," she said to Letty Mann, "and tell them we're here? They wouldn't want John not to be properly announced."

"Oh no, Miss Heron," said the little woman. "Of course Mr. Broome has to be properly announced."

Her manner seemed meek enough and her voice was what John thought of as shabby genteel. But to his sensitive ear, particularly attuned at this moment to any affront, it sounded subtly mocking, as if she had summed him up at a glance and placed him with relentless accuracy into the exact slot of the social hierarchy from which he came. He made an involuntary grimace and drew in his breath with a sharp little sound and hoped that Alice had not heard it.

"It's as bad as the dentist," he murmured to her as they

stood outside the door through which Letty, temporarily abandoning the tea-trolley, had disappeared. "Or the headmaster's study."

Alice giggled nervously and he stretched out a hand to catch hold of her own.

"No," she whispered fiercely, recoiling in panic. "We're only casual friends. For God's sake don't forget."

He had no chance to reassure her, for Letty flung wide the door and exposed them to the bright lights of the big drawing-room. John moved forward like an automaton, grinning idiotically, feeling as if his hands were the size of legs of lamb. The rich Persian carpet seemed to go on for ever; the tall figure standing in front of the ornate fireplace at the far end seemed miles away.

"Welcome, Mr. Broome," he heard a deep voice say, and he felt a firm clasp of the hand. His own must have raised itself of its own accord. "Alice has told us about you. Very kind of you to take the trouble to come and visit a couple of old fogeys. Young folks nowadays have usually got better things to do."

"Not at all. It's a great pleasure," muttered John, not knowing what he was saying, and mentally cursing Alice for omitting, among all her warnings, to tell him that her uncle was such a stunner to look at. Over six feet tall, straight as a rod for all his eighty years, with startlingly blue eyes and the head of a Roman emperor, topped by a glossy crown of dead-white hair.

Suddenly, quite unbidden, the words of one of Emily's most passionate love lyrics came into his mind, and with them a thought so shattering that he felt as if his excited trembling must be visible to all around him. The Unknown Beloved, the man to whom the poems were addressed, whose identity still remained a total mystery to the growing number of students of her work. Could it possibly be . . . ? Surely not. No one had been aware, up till now, that Sir Roderick Heron had ever been acquainted with Emily Witherington at all, and according to Alice they had been, at the very most, casual friends.

Casual friends. Just as he and Alice were pretending to be casual friends. It was no good: the thought had seeded itself in his mind and nothing would uproot it now. Meanwhile he must take a grip on himself and behave as he ought to.

"You're looking a little pale, my dear," he heard the old man say to Alice. "Too many late nights, perhaps, now that we are no longer keeping an eye on you."

"Oh no," protested Alice quickly. "I'm fine. Truly I am." She turned to smile at John and then looked back at her uncle. "John's working with Professor Woodward," she went on. "He's writing a book in the Victorian poets series."

"Ah yes." John received the full force of the blue eyes. "The young scholar from the north. There are quite a number of them in Oxford nowadays, I believe. And plenty of black faces about too, and not only at Balliol. Times have changed. I trust you are enjoying your studies, Mr. Broome?"

"Yes," said John. "Yes, thank you very much. Sir," he added, against all his egalitarian principles and very much against his will.

He was hypnotized by the eagle face and the brilliant eyes, and gave a visible start when he heard a new voice say: "You have hogged the limelight for long enough, Roderick. It is time your wife was introduced to this most interesting young man."

"You are right as usual, my dear," said Sir Roderick, and taking John's arm, he turned him round to face a winged chair at the other side of the fireplace. In its great upholstered depths sat a small bent figure. John looked down on another aquiline face and crown of white hair, but the eyes were dark brown this time, and the skin like wrinkled parchment. Lady Heron, Alice's Auntie Belle, looked her eighty years and more.

"You must excuse me from rising," she said. "I am a martyr to arthritis and my powers of movement are somewhat curtailed."

"Alice did tell me," said John, gently taking the dry and twisted hand. "Shall I bring up a chair?"

"Indeed you shall," she replied tartly, "since I cannot do it myself and Roderick would not deign to and Letty would certainly drop it, and Alice, of course, must now be considered a visitor in this household."

John found an upright chair and seated himself at Lady Heron's side. She seemed to him to be just very slightly less alarming than her husband, and if he talked to her for a while perhaps he could assemble his wits for the main assault.

"So you are John Broome from Leeds," she said when a table with cups and plates had been placed before them. "You have parents, I suppose?"

"A father."

"And mother?"

"Lost her," said John briefly.

The old lady twisted her body round with an effort and her dark eyes looked piercingly at John round the wing of the chair.

"You mean she's dead? How extraordinarily squeamish young people are about such things nowadays. Death is nothing to be ashamed of, young man. It is a very near relation to us all."

"I'm sorry," said John, taking a gulp of tea.

"The—er—loss, perhaps, is of a somewhat painfully recent date?"

"I'd rather," said John desperately, holding a hand to his mouth as he choked on a crumb, "not talk about it if you don't mind."

"By all means. It will spare me the hypocrisy of pretending to be distressed about a person of whom I know nothing. We will talk about my niece—or rather my husband's great-niece, since she is the granddaughter of my husband's younger brother, General Sir Francis Heron, and her father was also a serving officer, of course. When did you first meet Alice?"

Lady Heron took a cucumber sandwich and gobbled it up with the unconscious greed of old people who have few creature pleasures left.

"A few weeks ago," said John, trying to look completely unmoved by this account of Alice's ancestry while at the same time mentally reminding himself of the difference between baronets and knights bachelor. He glanced across the room, wondering how much longer he was to be left at the mercy of Auntie Belle. Alice was crouched on a stool at her uncle's feet, intent on what he was saying, while Letty, at his other side, looked up at him with an expression of open adoration on her face. There was no help to be had there.

He turned to face Lady Heron again. "Alice helped Professor Woodward entertain his research students at the beginning of term sherry party," he explained. "I was rather nervous, and she was very kind and made me feel at ease."

"She was unlike the girls back home, perhaps," said Lady Heron with such a knowing look and such a wealth of insinuation in her voice that John felt himself turning scarlet. If she had accused him outright of being a social climber and after Alice's money he could not have felt more uncomfortable. Feeble as Lady Heron looked, he was beginning to understand why Alice had described her as terrifying, and he was also beginning to feel that even the most staggering revelations about the life and death of Emily Witherington could not make up for such agonizing moments as these. And this was only the start. The old man himself lay ahead.

John heard himself give a silly little laugh and make some remark about how nice it was that Professor Woodward had Alice as a part-time secretary.

"He comes from your part of the country, I believe," said Lady Heron. "But he has been in Oxford a long time. I cannot honestly say that I am conscious of any rough edges when in Professor Woodward's presence. We quite understand that Alice wanted something to do to occupy her mind, but we would not have wished her to work with an uncultivated sort of person."

This time John was a little more prepared and was able to reply with some spirit that from his own knowledge of Alice, she would not have been happy in a commercial job. Lady Heron, apparently a little taken aback by his rapid recovery from his discomfiture, turned her attention to the companion-help.

"Letty, Letty, are you so besotted with the words of wisdom that are falling from Sir Roderick's lips that you do not perceive that both Mr. Broome and I have empty teacups?"

"Oh dear. I'm so sorry, Lady Heron. No, don't you trouble, Miss Alice—oh no, no, indeed no, John, I mean Mr. Broome. You stay there. Lady Heron wants to talk to you."

The little woman's flutterings were painfully embarrassing to witness and yet John had a disagreeable suspicion that, were he himself in a position of authority over Letty, he would scold and bully her too. As Alice had said, she seemed born to be a victim and there was no helping her.

Like many another oppressed and feeble creature, she would snap viciously at the helping hand. Besides, from his own precarious situation there was nothing he could do. A working-class boy floundering hopelessly out of his depth in an upper-class household, with a great personal favour to ask of his host, and falling hopelessly in love with the young lady of the house—why, he was only just hanging on by the skin of his teeth himself. He could do nothing for the unfortunate Miss Mann.

"Delicious cakes, Letty my dear," said Sir Roderick with magnificent condescension after taking a bite at one of them. "Definitely one of your better efforts. Don't you think so, Belle?"

His eyes turned to the shrunken little figure of his wife. John saw her look back at him with an intensity that was somehow shocking in one so old. Evidently the passion of hatred was longer-lived than the passion and pleasures of love. For a moment the two old people glared at each other and then they both looked towards Letty, who was standing with the silver teapot in one hand and a plate of cakes in the other, her unprotected face as red as John's had been a minute or two ago. There was no way in which she could escape; she was like a mouse caught between two most ferocious cats.

"Letitia Mann," said Lady Heron with the little writhing of the mouth that did service for a smile, "subscribes to the belief that the way to a man's heart is through his stomach. She aims high and she never gives up trying. What is your opinion, Mr. Broome? Could you find it in your conscience to—er—dispose of your wife in favour of a more proficient cook?"

John began to stammer something, looked hopelessly at Alice, and then dried up completely.

"I don't think John is very fussy about his food," said

Alice with such arch, unnatural brightness that John scarcely recognized her voice.

"Indeed?" Sir Roderick raised an eyebrow in polite disbelief. "He has perhaps higher things on his mind?"

John heard himself give his feeble laugh again. The tension in the room had become intolerable. He felt totally incapable of making any further effort whatever and it looked as if Alice had shot her last bolt too. With a sort of appalled curiosity he waited to see what would happen next. Was Lady Heron openly going to accuse her husband and her companion of conspiring to bring about her death? It looked horribly like it.

He glanced round the room as if seeking a way to escape, and saw the door, which was slightly ajar, slowly open wider. The effect was disconcerting and even creepy. There was no breeze; as far as he knew there was not another human being in the house. Emily's ghost, he thought, trying to fix his mind on the reason for his being in this frightful situation at all; Emily's ghost is hanging over us.

Round the edge of the door appeared a furry head, tiger-striped. Then a sleek, sinuous body with similar markings, and finally a thick tail, held upright and waving slightly at the tip. All eyes in the room turned to the door.

"Ah," said Sir Roderick with a long exhalation of breath. "Here's Quizzy."

"Quizzy," murmured Lady Heron in soft, caressing tones. "Good boy, then, come here." She patted her knee with her crippled hand.

"Quizzy!" cried Alice and Letty almost in unison, shrill with relief.

The tension in the room was miraculously dispersed. It was as if the cat had acted as a lightning conductor. He sat down on the carpet just inside the door, gave a quick lick to the base of his tail, and then stood surveying the five people present in a disdainful manner, his fine tiger-head moving slowly from side to side.

"The cream, Letty," said Sir Roderick with an air of command more suited to a general addressing his troops than to a tea-party.

Letty poured cream from the silver jug into one of the Crown Derby saucers and handed it to Sir Roderick, who lowered it to the floor and then twitched his fingers encouragingly at the animal. Lady Heron, Letty and Alice, all proceeded to hold out their hands to summon the cat. The suspense mounted; it was like watching a roulette-wheel. To whom would the cat go first?

"Come on, Quizzy," said John, reluctant to be left out, and fascinated by the behaviour of this creature who was the focus of so many human passions.

With a mixture of surprise and gratification he saw the cat walk straight across the carpet towards him, stare up at his face and let out a loud mew before rubbing against his leg. John bent down, glad to hide his face, conscious that all eyes in the room were now turned towards himself. Later on he swore to Alice that the cat winked at him before trotting over to lap up the cream and finally jumping on to Lady Heron's lap. She gave an involuntary little cry as the leap disturbed a painful spot on her leg, and then she settled down to coo over the animal and bury her twisted fingers in the thick fur.

It was both sickening and pitiful, and John tried not to look at her. In fact the whole situation was rather sickening. The superbly handsome old man, the spiteful suspicious old wife, the middle-aged woman who adored the old man and hated the old woman, and who probably had all sorts of hopes and dreams and ambitions of her own. It was like some ghastly parody of the eternal triangle, ludicrous and revolting because they were too old for such antics. And the very fact that it was taking place in such an opulent setting made it even worse. Rich, titled people, with a great variety of life experience behind them—was this what they were reduced to in their closing years? Getting at each other through the medium of the wretched domestic help, pouring out their frustrations upon a nice little tabby cat?

"Why did you call him Quizzy?" asked John, wondering how on earth he was ever going to get round to the subject of his own work. "Is it because he is exceptionally curious?"

Alice answered him. "It was my doing," she said. "We got him as a kitten when I was about six years old. I christened him Quizzy, didn't I, Uncle Rod?"

"Yes, my love," said the old man absent-mindedly. He was glancing at his watch and seemed to be a bit fidgety. Did this mean it was time to go, wondered John, and without even the slightest reference to the object of his visit? Desperation drove him to action.

"I expect Alice has explained to you, sir," he said, surprising even himself by the firmness of his voice, "that I'm doing the book about Emily Witherington in this series that Professor Woodward is editing."

He paused, too shattered by his own audacity to be capable of more. But Sir Roderick appeared not to have heard him. He was looking at his watch again and making impatient little gestures at Letty, who was fussing round the tea-trolley.

"Ten past eight the programme begins," he said peremptorily. "We shall want the trays put ready and the room arranged by eight o'clock at the very latest. Don't you think you'd better be getting on with it now?"

"Oh dear, yes, of course," babbled Letty. "I thought some hot soup would be nice as it's rather a chilly evening—"

"And I shall want my shawl," said Lady Heron. "I feel a draught at my back when we move my chair round."

The three of them continued to talk with great animation, continually interrupting each other, and John found himself free to have a quiet word with Alice.

"What's all this about?" he asked.

"Television panel-game," she replied. "*Saturday Night Quiz*. It's a weekly ritual. They wouldn't miss it for the world. They're like children at a party."

"How extraordinary," murmured John. "That ghastly drivel."

His disillusionment was now complete.

"You'll get nothing on Emily now," whispered Alice. "But cheer up. You'll be invited again. You've made a hit with Auntie."

"I can't have. She's been tearing me to shreds."

Alice smiled at him. "The cat," she said.

"Oh." Light dawned on John and his spirits began to revive a little. If the formidable Lady Heron had taken a liking to him because he had been lucky enough to make friends with the cat, then there might be some hope for him after all. And the next moment his prospects looked even brighter. The arrangements for the evening's entertainment having evidently been completed, Sir Roderick was once more free to attend to his guest.

"I beg your pardon, Mr. Broome," he said, beaming at John and speaking with a wealth of old-fashioned courtesy, "for being so abominably rude as to break off in the middle of our conversation. Alice will no doubt have explained to you the reason."

He paused, and John wondered uneasily whether his conversation with Alice could possibly have been over-heard. Sir Roderick's eagle eyes missed nothing, and his hearing seemed to be equally acute. But they hadn't said anything that they oughtn't. Or had they? In any case it seemed safest to keep quiet now. He didn't mind admitting to himself that he was scared stiff of the old tyrant. It didn't help at all to know that Sir Roderick was an avid viewer of one of the worst inanities on the television screen. A dozen revelations of such weakness would still make no difference. He stood four-square on the unassailable fortress of centuries of domination and he wasn't going to budge for anybody, least of all for a student from a provincial university who had nothing in the world but what nature had given him and who had had the temerity to fall in love with his niece.

They stood confronting each other, the old man and the young, the past and the future; they were much the same height, their eyes were almost on a level. The pause lasted for longer than any normal pause in conversation ought to last, and in the end it was the young man who gave way.

"She said you usually watch television on Saturday evenings," said John, "so I think I had better say good-bye now."

Sir Roderick's face broke into the indulgent smile of one who knows that he has scored a moral victory. He took John by the arm and guided him back to his chair.

"There's no need for you to hurry away just yet," he said. "I had to get Letty moving as she's inclined to be dilatory. She's a trifle peeved, I fear, because we don't suggest she should come and sit with us. But my wife and I do like to have an occasional hour by ourselves. You will understand this, I am sure."

John murmured his assent, unable as he did so to refrain from glancing towards the door, through which Letty was manoeuvring the tea-trolley. There was no doubt at all that she had heard what Sir Roderick had said, for he had taken no trouble to lower his voice. John found himself yet again mentally shrugging off Letty's troubles. It was horribly humiliating to be in her position, but after all it was her own choice. She could easily find another job if she wanted to, for good cooks were always in demand. If she chose to hang on here in the hope of one day becoming Lady Heron then it was her own fault if she got badly bruised in the process.

The room felt more comfortable after Letty had left it. Alice resumed her place on the stool, Lady Heron fondled the cat, and Sir Roderick devoted his attention to John.

"You were asking me something, I believe, when I was discourteous enough to interrupt you."

"Yes," said John hopefully. "About my poet, the one I'm writing about."

"Ah yes. Emily Dickinson, did you say? Wasn't she an American? I'm afraid I'm very ignorant about poetry, but I have certainly heard the name."

"No sir, not Dickinson. Emily Witherington is the one I'm writing about."

As he spoke the magic name John had the impression that a slight sound came from the direction of Lady Heron's chair. He glanced round, but could see no sign of her having taken any interest in the conversation. Her head was bent low over the purring cat and she was murmuring, "That's my good little boy, that's my precious."

John looked away again to see Sir Roderick leaning back in his chair, one elbow resting on the arm and the hand pressed to the side of his head, frowning as if with the effort to remember.

"Witherington," he repeated slowly. "That's a name I seem to have heard too." He lowered his hand and ruffled Alice's hair. "Not bad for an old 'un who knows nothing of poetry, is it, Alice?"

"No, darling." She smiled up at her uncle, and in the midst of all his excited anticipation, John felt a stab of quite irrational jealousy that this smile was not for himself. "But then you are not nearly such a Philistine as you like to pretend," she went on. "Are you, Uncle Rod?"

"Well, my dear." He was very complacent now. "I do know my Tennyson, if nothing else. We were brought up on him, you know. But I don't suppose any of you youngsters nowadays have a good word to say for him."

"As a matter of fact I rather like Tennyson," began John and then stopped abruptly. This wasn't what he wanted at all. A moment ago he had been on the verge of hearing something about Emily Witherington and now suddenly they were on a different tack. How had it happened? Could Sir Roderick deliberately have contrived the switch? Surely not; Alice had taken part in it too.

"Do you now?" Sir Roderick leaned forward in his eagerness. "I'm glad to hear it. Which is your favourite poem? 'Enoch Arden'? 'Maud'?"

Helplessly John resigned himself to a discussion of these masterpieces. The old man's views were in fact well worth hearing, but this wasn't what he had come for. The big grandfather clock in the corner ticked away the minutes. Any moment now it would be made plain that the time for departure had arrived.

"Do you think," he said desperately in a slight pause in the discussion, "that Emily Witherington was trying to imitate Tennyson when she wrote 'Love in the Arbour of Roses'?"

"'Love in the Arbour of Roses,'" repeated Sir Roderick, his face unmoved except for a return of the slight frown. "I don't think I know that poem."

You damned well do, said John to himself; you know more about that poem than anyone, living or dead, has ever known or will ever know except the author herself. For he was now as convinced as if he had read dozens of learned treatises on the subject, that sitting placidly across the room from him now was the cause and inspiration of Emily's beautiful love lyrics, and he was equally certain that there was no conceivable way of ever getting Sir Roderick to admit it. Would he himself feel embarrassed, he wondered, if he was the object of a girl's poetic expressions of passion? Well, perhaps he would. It would be rather like being taken for a gigolo. Usually it was the other way round; the male poet writing verses about his lady-love.

He quoted a few lines from the poem, very softly. Sir Roderick shook his head. "No. I'm sorry, my boy. They mean nothing to me."

"But you did meet Emily Witherington once or twice, didn't you, Uncle?" prompted Alice gently. "Auntie told me they used to live farther up the Banbury Road."

"That's right." Sir Roderick lifted a forefinger and his face came to life as with the excitement of returning memory. "That's right. That painter fellow—her brother, wasn't he? Don't you remember, Belle? We used to play tennis there occasionally. It was a most ill-organized household. Never a meal on time, and books and music and easels and paints all over the place."

He rose to his feet.

"It's come back to me now. Couldn't think who you were talking about at first."

He held out a hand. "Glad to have met you, Mr. Broome. Best of luck with your studies."

John took the hand. "Thank you, sir. If I could possibly trouble you once more—some time when you've a little more time to spare—"

Again they stared at each other, and John saw the fine eyebrows rise in ironic amusement. "Time, my dear chap, is what I have most of. The burden of retirement. Come along again. Fix it up with Alice. My wife and I will be very pleased to see you. We miss young life about the house since Alice left us."

John's thanks and farewells were much too effusive and were barely articulate from nervousness and excitement. Alice got him out of the house at last. At the corner of the road he stopped and hugged her, lifting her off her feet.

"Darling, darling, it's coming! The glorious future you've mapped out for me. Fancy the old boy turning up trumps at last! I say, what a stunner he is. My God, if I could look like that at eighty!"

She tried to cool his enthusiasm as soon as he had put her down and she had regained her breath.

"We've done far better than I'd dared to hope," she said, "but don't count your chickens yet, John. Uncle Rod is a very wily old bird. He'll twist you round his little finger and put you neatly aside if you aren't very careful and you won't even realize that he's doing it. He may tell you something useful about Emily and he may not. But at least he doesn't actually dislike you. I think he rather admires you for standing up to him."

"Have I been standing up to him?" asked John. "I feel as if I've been steam-rollered."

Alice laughed happily and took his arm. "You don't know what being steam-rollered means," she said. "You ought to see most of the boys who come to the house. They're grovelling on the carpet after the first five minutes. You're a hero. You're wonderful. And I love you."

— 3 —

Letty Mann stood outside the closed door of the drawing-room and listened for the lively tune that signified the start of *Saturday Night Quiz*. Then she ran up to her room, which was at the side of the house on the first floor, took a rusty key from a little box of odds and ends, and tiptoed across the landing to Lady Heron's room. There was not much risk that they would hear her footsteps from the drawing-room below, since they were always so absorbed in the programme, but you couldn't be too careful.

The rusty key opened the great mahogany wardrobe, whose legitimate key was kept in the little velvet bag that hung from Lady Heron's wrist and from which she was never parted day or night. Letty checked for spy-traps such as hairs or threads of cotton tucked round the lock, but found none. It looked as if Lady Heron had as yet no suspicion of what her companion-help did during the time when she had the run of the house without danger of interruption. The programme lasted only forty-five minutes, but Sir Roderick and Lady Heron always had a furious quarrel about its contents when it was over, so that Letty could count on nearly an hour of freedom.

First of all she slipped on the sable coat and admired herself in the long mirror. It suited her far better than it did the rightful owner, who could not wear it now because her frail body was unable to bear the weight of the fur. Then came the real business of the evening: the old letters. They were stuffed into an ebony workbox that stood on the shelf at the bottom of the wardrobe, and since they had only appeared the previous week and it looked as if this was only a temporary hiding-place until her ladyship could discover a better, Letty wasted no more time before getting down to reading. They were a wonderful find, because up till now she had not come across any private papers in this household; only bills and circulars and little letters concerning repairs to the car and boring things like that. The drawers of the desk in Sir Roderick's little den next to the dining-room were always kept locked, and Letty did not think she would have the courage to look into them even if she did find an old key that fitted; but Lady Heron's sanctum was not quite so unassailable, and it would be possible to think up an excuse for being there if need be.

With a little sigh of pleasurable anticipation she sat down on the yellow bedspread with the black box beside her and took out the letters. She was about two-thirds of the way through. They lay in neat piles on her lap, those already read and the joys yet to come. She picked up a lilac envelope with "To R. E. Heron, Esquire" written on it in a flowing feminine hand. At first glance it looked as if it was going to be like all the others—the most passionate love letters that one could ever imagine, far better than anything in the romantic mystery stories that Letty loved to read. But after the date and the words "My own beloved Roddy," and the usual remarks about "the inexpressible joy of being with you yesterday," this letter took a somewhat different course.

"But I am deeply concerned," it went on, "about a disgusting rumour that I heard this morning, about you and I.M. Tell me it is false, my darling. I cannot rest until I have once more the assurance of your love. I pace the room, I embrace the air as if I were embracing you. Tell me quickly, bring me once more to my ease. I shall go tomorrow towards sunset to our own secret place, walking with eager steps, revelling in all those beauties of nature that we have so often gazed on together, and never will the grass be greener or the air purer or the birds sing more sweetly, than when I find in our own dear sylvan post office the words penned in your dear hand—that precious message saying that you still love your own, your very own and ever-loving, E."

The postscript ran as follows: "I shall slip this letter into your hand this evening when we meet at A's. Please return it to me at the first opportunity as you have all my others. I will then destroy it myself. I always do this, since a premature discovery of our love would serve no useful purpose."

But she didn't destroy it, said Letty to herself, laying the letter on the bigger pile and taking up the next one; she kept the lot of them, and somehow or other they came into the possession of Lady Heron without Sir Roderick's knowledge. Either he had been a lot more trusting and less canny in his young days, or else he was so deeply in love himself that it had made him careless and indiscreet. The thought of Sir Roderick young and deeply in love was very disturbing to Letty, because she fully believed herself to be deeply in love with the old Sir Roderick at the present day. It was not purely for ambition, for love of money and rank, that she was determined to supplant the present Lady Heron before many more months had elapsed. The trouble was, how? Poison? They were all very fond of strong curry. Would its flavour hide the taste of a poison?

Letty put the problem aside for the moment and applied herself to the next letter. This really was a beauty. Evidently the reassurance that the writer had asked for had not been forthcoming.

"How can you be so mean and deceitful," it began furiously, "after we agreed to have no secrets from each other? Is she more beautiful than I, more spiritual, more gifted? I only seek to know. Prove to me that you have found one more worthy of your love and I will plead no more. Prove that you have found a better and I will let you go for ever, though you take with you my heart's blood and the sight of my eyes and the strength of my hand. Prove that she is my superior, prove it! But if it is for any other reason, if it is because her father is a scholar of high renown and mine was but a vagabond poet, if it is because your own father and mother think she would be—oh hideous phrase!—such a suitable match, then—"

Here Letty was obliged to turn the page. She did so with a little gasp of anticipation. It was as good as a film or a play. She could hear the writer's voice in her own mind, rising in its passion. Letty's hard little core of common sense told her that the writer was working herself up into a frenzy, revelling in her own drama, and yet she was quite carried away by it and oblivious of her surroundings and of the passage of time.

"—then I will destroy you and destroy her too," Letty read as she turned the page. "I am only a poor weak woman but I am not without friends, and my voice is not quite unknown. My own poor poet's pen still wields some power. The choice is yours and I am yours, for ever, if you will it."

"Well of all things! How could she destroy him?"

Letty spoke the words aloud, her eyes glittering with excitement, her fingers tremblingly propping up the letter against the little piles that lay on her lap.

In any case she had not destroyed them, because there they both were now, watching television downstairs in the drawing-room. So what could have happened? Had the girl killed herself for love? Somehow Letty did not think so. The voice was desperate but not a defeated one. It might threaten suicide but would not carry out the threat. Murder now. That was different. The girl who had written those letters was perfectly capable of murder.

It was terribly tempting to overrun the time and read some more, particularly since there might not be another chance. Letty sat hesitating, the letter in her hands, caution and curiosity warring within her. It was not just that she was dying to know the end of the story, but that she had the feeling that she might be on the brink of a discovery that could be turned to her own advantage. Letty was shrewd enough in her own way, for all her day-dreaming, and years of servitude in the intimacy of other people's homes had given her an ability not only to recognize the subtlest of social distinctions but also great skill at probing into dark corners, and an unerring instinct for discovering those facets of family life that the family would prefer to forget.

Up till now she had never actually attempted to make any use of her secretly-acquired knowledge beyond stirring up trouble between members of a household by a little judicious tactlessness at suitable moments. Sometimes she was scarcely conscious that she was doing it, and none of her employers had ever been able to pinpoint, under her cringingly obliging manner, any evidence of evil intent. She had always had impeccable references and yet every household in which she had worked had been relieved to see her go. Letty was usually glad to go too. When she had cracked the nut and found the kernel not worth the tasting she was anxious to move on to the next one. But this time she was going to stop, for there was a glittering prize within her reach, and after this the ordinary middle-class household would seem more dull and insipid than ever.

As she sat there, lost in wonder at the thought that her own life might be taking on the nature of a romance, she felt something soft brush against her hand. She hit out instinctively; there was a loud squeal and sharp claws tore into her wrist. She dropped the letter, pressing the other hand to the pain, and twisted round to look into the tiger-face and mysteriously reproachful eyes of Quizzy.

"You devil, you!" she cried. "Sneaking in like that. You'd tell on me if you could but you can't speak so I'm safe."

The scratch had gone deep; when Letty drew away the fingers of the other hand she saw that they were covered in blood.

And then she once more cried aloud with horror. On the lilac-coloured page that lay in her lap there was a deep red stain; still wet but rapidly spreading and drying. Sixty years after the ink of those impassioned words had first dried, it had been moistened afresh by another woman's blood.

Letty sprang up in a panic and the little piles of letters cascaded on to the floor. She picked them up and stood at the end of the bed shaking so much that her knees nearly gave way, while Quizzy crouched on the yellow bedspread and watched her with his all-seeing eyes.

The minutes ticked away. There was a loud swell of music from the room below. The viewers would hold their angry post-mortem and then they would be calling for her. Impossible to remove the bloodstain and sort out the letters and put them back in time. There was only one thing to be done. She shut the black box and replaced it on the shelf, locked the wardrobe with the rusty key, smoothed down the bedspread—thank God there was no bloodstain there—and made off with the letters to her own room, leaving the cat in possession, motionless, inscrutable, sphinxlike.

Later that night, with the door of her bedroom locked and an excuse ready in her mind should anyone discover it, Letty lay in bed with a pile of envelopes on the table beside her, in a state of agitation greater than she had ever known in her life, and thinking harder than she would have believed possible. It far exceeded the very best of her romantic thrillers, this story of love and attempted revenge that was unfolding before her eyes. But unlike the thrillers it had no end: only a big question mark.

Letty read and re-read, and thought and thought, bringing to bear on the mystery every little scrap of family history that she had discovered while residing in the Heron household, scraps picked up from the old people themselves, from Alice, from Jimmy, from Lionel Heron-Renfrew, heir to the baronetcy, and from other visitors to the house, right down to the visit of that young fellow of Alice's this very afternoon. Now he ought to be able to help, if anybody could. Letty had guessed the object of John's visit from earlier remarks of Alice's that she had overheard, but it was not until she had read the remainder of the letters that the whole thing fell into place and the full implications of his introduction into the household dawned on her.

Good heavens, if she was right in her suspicions, and if this boy was going to ask Sir Roderick to tell him everything he knew about the young lady poet whose first name began with an E . . . ! Well! Letty's mind could find no words adequate for such an extraordinary situation. None of her favourite authors had ever thought up anything like that. It just showed you that truth was stranger than fiction, and it was plain that this young fellow hadn't the least idea in the world of what a hornet's nest he was walking into, and neither had Alice, or she would not have dragged him into it.

Whatever would sir Roderick do? A gentlemen placed in that position in the old days would have let the dogs loose on the snooping investigator, but one couldn't do that nowadays, because the boy did seem to have some sort of credentials, however low-class he was and even though he spoke with a common Yorkshire accent. Besides, there were no dogs here, only that spoiled brute of a cat, whom Letty was determined to get even with some day.

How far would the youngster persist? If it came to a battle of wits he couldn't begin to match up to the old one. Sir Roderick would play around with him for a while and then toss him over his shoulder without turning a hair. Would one such tossing be enough? Letty rather hoped so. If the boy had been a different sort they might have worked profitably together, he being a scholar and doing the brainwork, she having the practical experience and knowing the lie of the land. They could have made their fortunes together, she with her baronet, he with his heiress. But she knew his sort and knew he wouldn't play. Touchy and stuck-up and proud, like so many of these working-class lads when they got a bit above themselves; despising all the little subterfuges that those of humble station had to resort to in order to hold their own in a tough and hostile world.

She might try to sound him out if she got the chance, but on the whole she believed it would be best to keep her own counsel in the hope that he would soon retreat and leave her in full possession of the field.

4

It was a bright warm April afternoon when John turned into Blenheim Close to keep his momentous appointment with the man whom he had come to think of as Emily Witherington's Unknown Beloved, although he realized that not for a moment must he let it be seen that this thought was in his mind. He was whistling "Sally in our Alley" as he walked along, partly to keep up his courage, partly through sheer joy of youth and health and hope and love. The daffodils were out in every garden and the lilac bushes were already showing their tight little bright green leaf-buds.

As he came near to Number Eleven he heard the loud squawking of cats' quarrel, and saw a black tail rapidly disappearing round the corner of the neighbouring house and a small striped form sitting triumphantly on the boundary wall. John laughed and stretched out a hand.

"Well done, Quizzy," he said. "That's right. You defend your own."

There was something agreeably cosy and reassuring

about being welcomed by the cat, and it raised John's hopes of being one day welcomed into the family itself. The gulf was very wide, of course, much wider than he had realized before he came to know them, but after all this was a democratic age, and Alice loved him, and if Sir Roderick really did like people who could stand up for themselves, then what could be better than taking the opportunity to prove oneself, like the mythical heroes of old. If the testing consisted of a scholarly achievement instead of the slaying of a dragon, well, after all this was a peaceful and civilized world.

Such were John's thoughts as he tugged at the old-fashioned bell-rope, and his hopeful anticipation was only slightly dampened by the fact that it was Letty, and not Alice, who opened the door.

"They're expecting you," she said, looking up at him in her sly and knowing fashion.

"Yes, I know. I've come to tea."

"Lady Heron has not been at all well. Alice is staying here and looking after her."

"I know," said John again, with slight impatience. Letty was blocking his way into the hall and he was longing to get in and see Alice. "But I gather she's much better now."

"Oh you do, do you," said Letty with a little toss of the head as she stepped aside to let John pass. "Well, since you seem to know everything that's going on in this house you won't need me to give you any advice."

John stared at her. The genteel accent had slipped. Her tone had been rough and insolent. She would never have dared to talk to one of the Herons like that. Was this the real Letty? And if so, whatever had he done to earn her dislike?

Alice came out of the drawing-room and John's momentary discomfiture faded away.

"You're nice and early," she said cheerfully. "We'll have

tea at once if you're ready, Letty dear, because Auntie doesn't want to sit up much longer and Uncle wants to show John the garden afterwards as it's such a nice afternoon."

"It's all ready. I'll bring it in," said Letty, reverting to her normal voice but with a touch of sullenness.

Alice really does dislike her, thought John, watching the two women. Being Alice, she could never be openly unkind, but there was a great difference between the genuine warmth of Alice's greetings to John's elderly landlady when she visited him, and the forced brightness of her manner towards Letty. When he came into the drawing-room, however, he was so shocked by Lady Heron's appearance that he ceased to think about Letty or even about his forthcoming interview with Sir Roderick.

It seemed incredible that the old lady could look even more shrivelled and frail than she had looked before, but she certainly did so. The winged chair seemed bigger than ever; the oak walking-stick with which she tapped on the floor looked like a tree-trunk in her bloodless fingers. John shook hands with Sir Roderick, who was as usual commanding the hearth-rug, and sat down beside Lady Heron.

"I'm sorry to hear that you've not been well," he said gently. "I hope you'll soon be feeling better now that spring's come. It's a lovely day."

The dark eyes, clouded a little with sickness and pain, looked at him with an expression that he could not fathom.

"Spring is for the young," she said. And then, even more softly: "April is the cruelest month."

"Oh." John looked at her in some surprise. "Do you read T. S. Elliot?"

"And why not, pray?" There was a flash of her old spirit. "It's not every eighty-year-old who is stuck in the morass of Victorian sentimentality."

She directed one of her barbed looks at her husband, who

merely smiled benignly and welcomed the advent of the tea-trolley.

When the ritual of distributing the small tables and the cups and plates had been accomplished, Alice said: "Auntie used to tutor students for college entrance exams. And review poetry for the journals."

"Oh, really?" It was more than a polite expression of interest on John's part. It would be fascinating to know what this highly intelligent old lady, brought up in such a very different kind of society, thought of the literature of the mid twentieth century. He turned towards her with an inquiry on his lips, but the little flash had been no more than a last stray spark from a barely smouldering fire. Lady Heron was looking disgustedly at a small piece of toast that lay on her plate. Letty was standing nearby, holding a plate of appetizing-looking little delicacies just out of Lady Heron's reach.

"If the doctor says I can't have crab sandwiches then why do you make them?" grumbled the old lady. "You're doing it on purpose to spite me. Or to poison me. One or the other."

"You'll soon be feeling better, Auntie," said Alice soothingly, while her uncle did full justice to Letty's little savouries.

"Very tasty, my dear," he said.

It was a milder repetition of John's first visit. The tension was less only because Lady Heron had not the strength to exude the intensity of hatred that had characterized the previous occasion. But this time John's own sympathies were differently engaged; they were wholeheartedly with Lady Heron. Her husband and her companion were openly baiting her, and even Alice did not seem to be giving her as much support as she might have done.

Alice seemed to be in a reminiscent mood. She wandered over to the window-seat and rested a knee on it.

"The laburnum is going to be out early this year," she said. "I hope there's a lot of it. I love laburnum. Do you remember, Uncle Rod, how I used to sit here watching for you to come home when I was five years old and you were still going up to London three or four times a week?"

The old man glanced towards her and it seemed to John that for a brief moment there was a softer look on his face.

"Yes, my love," he said. "You were a funny little skinny thing. Nanny was always worried because she couldn't put an ounce of flesh on you."

"And on Sunday afternoons you took me into the Parks to feed the ducks on the round pond. I looked forward to that all the week."

There was a silence, not a tense silence this time, but a nostalgic one, heavy with memories. Even Letty stopped making the unnecessary little movements which made you feel as if you could never be truly at ease when she was in the room. Lady Heron's eyes were closed and she seemed to be sunk in upon herself. John looked across at Alice, still kneeling on the window-seat with her back to the room, and at the old man's face turned towards her. The ghost of Emily Witherington ceased momentarily to haunt him. Its place was taken by two other shadows—a tall, distinguished-looking gentleman in his mid sixties, with thick greying hair, and beside him skipped a funny, thin, serious-looking little girl, clutching at his hand as eagerly as fifteen years later she had clutched at John's, while the other small hand gripped a paper bag containing bread to feed the ducks. The ghosts caught at his heart and flooded it with a deep understanding that seemed at the same time to sweep away his own hopes.

Alice's great-uncle had been all in all to the little

orphaned girl. How could it have been otherwise? And he was all in all to her now, however much her adult mind might criticize him and her adult feelings rebel at his tyranny. She would never marry against his wishes. She would suffer and be torn apart, but in the end the old love would outweigh the new. For she was also everything to him, the brightness of his last years, the compensation for having no son and heir, no children of his own. Why, even behind those steely eyes and that imperious brow there lay a full measure of human grief and pain.

A deep melancholy settled upon the room, in sad contrast to the sunny daffodils in the spring garden beyond the window. The cruellest month, the cruellest time, thought John. It was as if they were all held fast in the grip of all the blighted hopes and unfulfilled desires of the dead past and of the future that was never to be.

At last Sir Roderick roused himself. "Here's Quizzy for his cream," he said, not heartily as on the previous occasion, but automatically, as if his mind was still elsewhere. Letty began to bustle again and the saucer was lowered to the floor. John watched the little pink tongue slip in and out as it rapidly demolished the rich liquid. How nice to be a cat, he thought; no agonizing over what is past and what is to come; just thoughtlessly gobbling up the nearest pleasure there is to hand.

When the saucer was empty the cat yawned and stretched and trotted over to his usual haven. John intercepted his leap on to Lady Heron's lap, lifting Quizzy up himself and placing him gently on the folds of the old lady's grey dress. She twisted her head round to thank him, and John caught an expression he had never thought to see in the angry old eyes. They looked misty and moist, and he had a glimpse of something soft and vulnerable that had built a thick armour of spite and ridicule around itself.

"It's surprising what a weight he is," said John, allowing Quizzy to pretend to bite his finger. "Although he's not a very big cat."

"You handle him very well," said Lady Heron. "Unlike Letty, who is the only person that Quizzy ever scratches. I wonder why?"

After a little desultory conversation Alice got up and came across to her aunt's side. "Shall I help you back to bed now, Auntie?" she asked. "I expect you're tired. Then Letty can clear away and Uncle can take John into the garden."

This was all according to plan. If someone had told John an hour ago that at this moment his thoughts would be less with Emily than with another woman, he would not have believed them. But it was in fact the case. He watched Alice put an arm round the old woman and ease her up from the chair. He would have liked to help too, but felt that it would be out of place for him to interfere. He would also have liked very much indeed to learn something of the life-story of Isabella Heron.

But Sir Roderick was summoning him and the moment he had hoped for had arrived. They walked past the kitchen and the downstairs cloakroom into the garden at the back of the house. At the far end of the big lawn a man was bending over a flower-bed.

"Jimmy!" called Sir Roderick in a loud voice.

"Yes sir!" The man straightened up and placed his heels together. He was slight in build and had a long melancholy face. He looked at John suspiciously as they approached and John was reminded of Letty's attitude towards him. It was plain that the domestic staff recognized instantly that John did not belong to the ruling classes and it looked as if they resented his appearance as a guest.

"Move that seat into the sun," said Sir Roderick. "Mr. Broome and I are going to sit here for a while."

"Yes, sir."

The little man pulled a rustic bench from the shade of a tall shrub out on to the gravel path. He seemed to be tough and wiry in spite of his age and build; nevertheless John found himself itching to go to his help. It seemed dreadful to let an old man wait on him like this. He was conscious that his host was eyeing him speculatively, and felt that this was some sort of test, trivial though the incident was. If he helped old Jimmy with the bench Sir Roderick would despise him; if he didn't help, he would dislike himself, because it was an essential part of his whole code of conduct and philosophy of life that the stronger should help the weaker.

In his nervousness he fell into the uneasy compromise of reaching out a hand to the back of the bench just as Jimmy had finished pulling it round. They collided awkwardly with each other; Jimmy gave John an offended look, and John found himself apologizing to his host's gardener under the amused stare of his host. There could not have been a worse beginning to the coming interview. The carefully prepared sentences and questions fled from his mind. He looked hopelessly at the retreating back of the gardener and found himself longing for the sight of a little tabby cat to bring him courage and help to break the ice.

"Well," said Sir Roderick, laying an arm along the back of the bench and crossing one immaculately clad leg over the other, "I believe you wanted to ask me something."

John plunged into a long rambling account of his work, of the sources he had been using to gain his information about Emily, his own assessment of her poems, and the gaps that needed filling if the story of her life was to be complete. He had just enough presence of mind left not to refer to the common assumption among literary critics, that Emily's finest love poems had been inspired by a real living person, but by the time he had stopped to draw breath and to wonder whether he was not boring his host to death, there was not much that his hearer had not learnt about John Broome's study of Emily Witherington.

"You see, I didn't want you to think I was pestering you for all sorts of little details that I could get from other sources," went on John. "It's awfully good of you to let me come and talk to you at all."

"Not at all," said Sir Roderick with a slight wave of the hand and a benevolent little inclination of the head. "It is most interesting to hear about her work. You seem to be making a very thorough job of it. I like good workmanship."

"The thing is," said John, suspecting sarcasm in these last remarks but rushing on hurriedly while his courage held, "that I have so few contemporary impressions of her. Her brother never married and the family seems to have died out completely except for very distant connections in Canada who never met her at all. If I could have just one contemporary opinion it would put the whole thing into perspective and make all the difference in the world to my book."

"I dare say it would," said Sir Roderick.

"Did you know her well?" continued John, eyeing him nervously as if the old man was a tiger about to spring.

Sir Roderick raised his eyebrows. "It depends what you mean by 'well'. In my young days it was always the lady's privilege to define the degree of acquaintance and I am perhaps rather out of touch with the standards of these less formal times. You would no doubt consider that you know my niece Alice 'well'?"

"Oh, I think so," said John, falling headlong into the trap

and belatedly trying to pull himself out. "At least, that is, I don't know whether any human being can ever be said truly to know another . . ."

He floundered about, feeling himself going as red as when Lady Heron had first questioned him about his parentage, and knowing that he was revealing his own feelings for Alice as plainly as if he had been shouting them from the housetops.

Sir Roderick continued to smile blandly but said nothing.

"Emily Witherington," said John desperately, getting a grip on himself again with a great effort. "Her death must have been a frightful shock to those who knew her."

"It was a shock," said Sir Roderick in a very sober voice. "A very great shock indeed."

"She was so young," said John, "and so lovely. At least she looks lovely in that photograph in the last volume of poems, the one in profile where she's sitting looking at a bowl of flowers. It's terribly sentimental of course, but it doesn't make her any the less lovely. Was she really as beautiful as that, sir?"

"I cannot recollect," replied Sir Roderick, "ever having seen the portrait to which you refer, so I cannot in honesty answer your question. She was, as far as I remember, generally regarded as a beauty among her acquaintance. Presumably I concurred in the general opinion, but I have had the good fortune to meet many beautiful women during the course of my life both at home and overseas, and you would not, I am sure, wish me to attempt to place them in a sort of league table."

"Of course not," said John shortly, in no doubt at all now about Sir Roderick's sarcasm, and feeling his own temper rising. Uncle is a frightfully tough nut, Alice had told him, with admiration as well as warning in her voice; he's a genius at making people lose control of themselves so that they tell him things they didn't mean to or resign their jobs when they didn't really want to at all. You'll just have to take a deep breath and count to ten if you feel you want to punch his nose.

John tried doing this now. Tough nut, he said to himself as he took the deep breath, was putting it mildly. The old devil would put the Spanish Inquisition to shame. With no hope now of ever learning anything new about Emily, but with some faint notion of trying to salvage some of his own self-esteem, he began to speak again.

"It must seem rather silly to you," he said, "that someone of my age should be so interested in somebody whom you regarded as a mere casual acquaintance who happened to write poetry. But it looks different from a distance, you know. Time lends enchantment. That sort of thing."

"Yes indeed," said Sir Roderick. "I quite appreciate your motives and your interest. There was such a thing as—what is the jargon term nowadays?—the 'generation gap' even when I was a boy. Every generation discovers it afresh, together with all the other aspects of human relationships that have been since the world began. And every one of us still has new things to learn, even when over eighty. I, for example, have just been experiencing for the first time in my life the extraordinary sensation of being told about the era of my youth by a youth who is scarcely older than I was then. It is very curious. My own memory paints a very different picture from that painted by the young historian. I wonder which one of us is nearer to the truth?"

John listened in silence, staring at the ground, no longer deceived by the old man's smooth, courteous tones. When they ceased he glanced up at his companion. There was the same ironic twist to the mouth, the same raised eyebrows, the same penetrating look from the brilliant eyes. Sir Roderick Heron's impenetrable mask. One could batter oneself against it for ever and only get more and more bruised in the process.

Poor Emily, he thought; poor Lady Heron; poor all the people who had had to work for him, poor everybody who ever had the misfortune to come up against this monumental granite slab of a man. Except, perhaps, for Alice. If Sir Roderick had an Achilles heel at all, then surely it must be Alice, but even she could not be of any help now. If she had been able to find out anything useful about Emily then she would have done so. But she hadn't, and neither had John himself.

He had told Sir Roderick practically everything he knew or suspected about the poet and had learnt precisely nothing in return. The whole business had been a complete shambles. He felt utterly routed in every direction, and worst of all, he had, for the moment at least, lost all faith in himself and his work and his future and in Alice's love for him.

Sir Roderick rose to his feet. "Shall we go in?" he said. "It's getting a little bit chilly out here, I think."

John stood up and accompanied him disconsolately across the lawn.

— 5 —

When they reached the square of crazy paving outside the back door, Sir Roderick paused and said: "You will stay and dine with us? My wife, I fear, will not come down again this evening, but my niece will be here and will no doubt welcome your presence. And Letty makes a very good curry. We are rather partial to strong curries in this household."

John murmured an acceptance because he had not the presence of mind to invent an excuse, much though he was longing to take his battered feelings away and nurse them in peace and solitude. What was the old devil up to now, he wondered dully; hadn't Sir Roderick achieved his object and stifled all enquiries about Emily Witherington for ever? And then it dawned on him. Of course that was only half of the exercise. The other half was no doubt to separate him from Alice, not by such crude methods as forbidding him to see her or openly disapproving of their friendship, for that would only have aroused Alice's resistance and welded them more closely together. Oh no, it had been much more carefully planned. The object was to make Alice herself have doubts about John, to make Alice herself the instrument of his final dismissal.

It was a brilliant piece of strategy and it was almost certainly going to succeed. Both halves of the exercise accomplished in one triumphant stroke. First of all raise John's hopes so that he was taken off his guard; then shatter both his hopes and his self-confidence so completely that he could not fail to show himself at his very worst—awkward, sulky, defensive; then finish off the job by making him sit through a formal dinner with Alice present to witness how feebly he was behaving. And Lady Heron, who John still believed was truly friendly towards him and who in any case would provide some protection by her mere presence, would not be there. Had Sir Roderick arranged that too? John wouldn't put it past him. He was capable of anything. He would stab you in the back with a warm gesture of good fellowship, offer you a poisoned cup with a hospitable smile on his lips.

Did Alice know all this? Probably, but she wouldn't be the first woman to have loved a beast—whether as a brother, husband, father or anything else. There was only one possible way to save himself in Alice's opinion. He must just go away, instantly, this very moment, without any excuse, any word of farewell. Swerve to the left, run round the side of the house, through the wrought-iron gate, and leave them all taken by surprise and guessing. Alice would come round. She would never be able to leave it just like that. And he could win her back to him, in his own time and in his own way, far from the paralysing presence of her uncle.

John felt all this, but his will was numb and his legs

refused to move. Sir Roderick was prodding with his stick at some grass growing up between the flagstones.

"Damn the fellow!" he exclaimed. "He's been using weedkiller again. I told him not to. Jimmy!" he roared. "Come here, Jimmy."

"Does it kill the flowers too?" asked John, unable to endure the tense silence.

"It's not the plants. They can be replaced. But there's only one Quizzy."

As they were talking, the cat emerged from under a shrub, ran up and sniffed at the white powder strewn on the flagstones, and then trotted off again, twitching his tail in disgust.

"He knows he mustn't eat it," said John in relief. Sir Roderick took no notice of him. He was scolding the old gardener, who had now arrived from the far end of the lawn.

"Where are you keeping the stuff?" he concluded.

"In the shed."

"Bring it here."

There was a silence while Jimmy fetched a black and yellow packet from the garden shed near the back door.

"I'll take charge of this," said Sir Roderick, taking the packet from Jimmy. "If you really have to use it, you must ask me."

He walked on into the house, John following him, but far enough behind to catch Jimmy's angry mutter.

"What's the guv'nor up to now? I've used it for years and the cat never touches it."

"You go ahead and help yourself to a drink," said Sir Roderick as John caught up with him outside the kitchen door, "while I put this away and see how the dinner is progressing."

And what happens now, John asked himself: weed-killer in the curry for everyone? Nothing seemed impossible with

Sir Roderick in charge, and at the moment he felt that he really didn't care.

But this mood of total defeat and dull acceptance was broken as soon as he came into the front hall. Alice emerged from round the stairs, where the telephone table stood; she was pale and agitated and scarcely looked where she was going.

"Darling!" John caught hold of her. "What's the matter?"

"I must go," she cried, disengaging herself. "Auntie's dreadfully ill. I've just rung the doctor and he's bringing a nurse along too."

She raced upstairs and he followed her, past caring now whether he was committing any social solecism in coming uninvited to the first floor of the house. At the top of the stairs he stood hesitating for a moment, and then moved towards the open door through which Alice had gone. A most extraordinary scene met his eyes. Lying in a white nightgown upon the yellow bedspread was the tiny, twisted little figure of Lady Heron, writhing and kicking and hitting out at Letty, who was trying to induce her to get between the sheets.

"Go away," she said in an angry voice. "Go away, you sneaking creature. Spy! Poisoner!"

Alice came forward and soothed her, pushing Letty aside, and gently lifting the old lady into bed. "Hush, Auntie," she murmured. "Don't excite yourself. You'll make yourself worse. Letty's not done you any harm."

"Oh yes, she has!" cried Lady Heron with surprising vehemence. "She's been snooping and she's going to poison me. She's been practising with aspirin and sleeping-pills to see if I notice the taste, and it'll be something worse next time if she can get away with it. And I know who's egging her on to do it. I know what they're up to—"

A fit of choking stopped the angry flow, and John saw the

old woman collapse into Alice's arms. Only for a moment, though. The dark eyes opened again and stared straight at him as he stood hovering in the doorway.

"Is that John Broome? Come here, John Broome. I want to speak to you."

John took a few steps forward into the room. Alice looked at him appealingly and Letty glared at him. The old woman in the bed had shut her eyes; her head had fallen sideways and her mouth drooped open. For a shocked second John believed that her end had come, and then he saw her hands move slowly over the bedspread, feeling for something.

"I wonder what she wants," murmured Alice, leaning over her.

"She wants the cat!" cried John, suddenly inspired. "She wants to stroke Quizzy."

Lady Heron opened her eyes and her lips twitched in acknowledgement. She raised a hand and beckoned John to come to her. Alice moved aside so that he could take her place.

"Shall I fetch him for you?" he asked. "I think he's in the garden."

"Not yet. Later." The old woman took his hand. "Go away, you!" she screamed at Letty. "I never want to see you again."

Letty folded her hands in front of her and looked at Alice for instructions. She said nothing, but her posture said plainly enough that in her opinion the old woman was mad and Alice must be treated like the mistress of the house now.

"I really do think it would be best if you would go," said Alice apologetically. "Thank you so much for helping me with her. I'm afraid it's delayed you with the dinner."

"All right," said Letty, going towards the door.

"Sir Roderick was looking for you just now to talk about dinner," John called after her. He could not help but feel sorry for the woman at this moment, whether or not Lady Heron's accusations had any foundations in fact. His own self-esteem had just taken such a mighty tumble that he had a fellow-feeling for anyone else in a similar predicament. But Letty did not take his intervention in the spirit in which it was offered. She paused on the threshold and gave him such a vicious look that he was quite startled. It was even more of a relief than usual when she finally left the room.

"Alice," said Lady Heron, who also looked relieved and even a little stronger after Letty's departure, "go after her and keep a watch on her. I want you to hear what she says to your uncle. And I want John alone for a moment. Hurry up. The doctor will be here soon."

The moment Alice had gone Lady Heron began to fumble at the tiny velvet bag that still hung round her wrist.

"Quick," she said. "The key's in here. Get it out for me."

John extracted a small key.

"The wardrobe," she said. "The bottom shelf. The black workbox. Take it out."

She was very excited now, speaking in short, breathless sentences, and leaning forward and reaching out with her arms as if trying to hasten on his movements.

"Is this it?" asked John, lifting up the black box. Memories of death-bed scenes from famous Victorian novels came into his mind and filled it with the wildest ideas. Was this her will? Was he to witness it? Or destroy it? Or was she thinking of leaving him some money because he had made friends with her cat?

"The letters," gasped Lady Heron. "Take them away. Stuff them into your pockets. All of them. Hurry up, hurry, hurry, hurry!"

Feeling not merely puzzled now, but rather unreal, as if he had indeed walked into the pages of a novel, John did as she told him. His trouser pockets held only a few of the envelopes, but his sloppy old jacket pockets were able to accommodate the rest. He crammed the last of them in and replaced the box and locked the wardrobe, to the accompaniment of increasingly agitated cries from the bed.

"What am I to do with them?" he asked in a whisper as he replaced the key in the velvet bag.

"Keep them in a safe place," she replied, a little calmer now, "but don't read them. Not yet. Promise me you won't read them."

She gripped the sheets and her eyes blazed up at him.

"I promise," said John.

"Only if I should die," she went on, lowering her eyes. "If you hear of my death you are to read them and take action."

"What action am I to take?" asked John, bending closer to catch her words, for her voice was now very faint.

"You've got brains," she replied. "And plenty of imagination. You'll think of something to do. I want it made public. I want him to be punished at last. I've kept quiet all these years because—"

She broke off and lay panting for a moment or two. John waited in a state of unbearable excitement and suspense, somewhat tempered by pity and concern.

"If I die," continued Lady Heron in a stronger voice, "it will be because he has encouraged that silly woman to poison me. He won't do it himself. He'll egg her on to do it for him and then he'll get rid of her, but she doesn't realize that, the fool. He's tired of me now because I'm too feeble to be worth tormenting and he'd like a last fling with someone else while there's yet time. Oh yes, you may well look amazed, but it won't be the first time an old man has turned some silly young woman's head. I don't know who it will be—does it matter? The thing is, he is not to get away with it. No, no, Alice is no good," she added, yet again answering John's unspoken thought. "She's so fond of her uncle that she'll try to hush it up, whatever it is. She'll pretend it hasn't happened. There's nobody else I can trust. I've nobody to rely on but you. Promise me."

The old woman pulled herself up by clutching the bedclothes and looked keenly into John's eyes. "Promise me," she said again.

"If only I knew what it was," said John slowly. It was one thing, he thought, frantically trying to assemble his wits, to promise a very sick woman not to read some letters, however urgent his own curiosity, but it was quite another to promise to act as her instrument of revenge on her husband, particularly when that husband was the terrifyingly formidable Roderick Heron, whom John felt he would never have the courage to tussle with again.

"You'll see when the time comes," said Lady Heron. The weary old eyes looked at him speculatively. "If you play your cards right you'll get Alice and her money too."

"Oh my God!" exclaimed John, and his own eyes pleaded with her. Whatever dynamite was this that she had persuaded him to conceal about his person?

"You're a good boy," she said softly, touching his hand. "I'd like to have had a son like you. I'd like you to marry Alice."

"I don't know what to say," he muttered, lowering his head. "I hate to make blind promises that I may not be able to keep even if I wanted to."

"You'll want to carry out this one," she said, "and you'll do it too, if you keep your wits about you."

She beckoned him nearer and a wicked look came into her eyes. "It's to do with your favourite poet, Emily

Witherington," she said, and fell back against the pillows again with a faint smile on her lips.

John leapt to his feet and clapped his hands to his bulging pockets. "My God, my God!" he cried loudly.

"Hush," she murmured. "Hurry up, now. I can hear the doctor's car. Get out of the house."

John rushed out of the room and down the stairs, feeling as guilty as if he were making off with the Crown Jewels. One half of him was frothing over with excitement; the other half wanted to throw the letters from him as if they had been a bomb and escape from this house, never to enter it again, Alice or no Alice, Emily or no Emily. The bell rang as he reached the bottom stair, and he nearly collided with Letty, who was coming from the kitchen to answer it. At the same moment Alice appeared in the door of the drawingroom, and Sir Roderick came out of his little den. They couldn't have timed it better had it been the ludicrous climax of some ghastly theatrical farce.

"Lady Heron asked me to post a letter," cried John wildly to the lot of them, and made a frantic dash for the front door.

He opened it to reveal a stout elderly man and a tall woman in dark grey standing together on the step.

"Excuse me," he cried, pushing roughly past them and leaving them staring indignantly after him.

A small tabby cat emerged from under the laburnum tree and gave a plaintive mew as John pulled open the gate.

"Sorry, Quizzy, not now," he muttered as he let the gate clang behind him.

And then he sprinted as he had not done since he won the quarter-mile in his last term at school.

6

Ten minutes later John was sitting panting on the bed in the main room of his basement flat, staring at the jumble of envelopes lying beside him and feeling grateful that both his landlady and Graham, the chemistry student who lived on the first floor, seemed to be out of the house. The struggle with his conscience could take place without fear of interruption. It lasted for some minutes, and the grounds of the arguments for not keeping his promise kept shifting.

If she really is dying, then it doesn't matter if I read the letters now or later, was his first thought. If her husband and Letty are really planning to poison her, then maybe if I read the letters I will learn something that will help me to stop them, was his second. Then came a rather more ignoble consideration: I don't suppose for a moment that I shall ever see her again so she'll never know that I've broken my promise. And then a rather more complicated piece of rationalization: if I am really going to try to expose her husband for her after she dies, then I can't do it on the spur

58

of the moment; it will need a great deal of thought and planning and preparation, and I can't do any of that until I know what it is that I'm going to expose.

There followed a moment when he wondered whether he ought to wait and consult Alice before taking any action at all, even though the old woman had more or less told him not to and had deliberately excluded Alice from the whole transaction. The thought was rejected almost immediately. If these letters contained anything detrimental to her uncle, Alice would insist on their being burnt at once, even if they held the answer to the mystery of Emily Witherington and were therefore a vital stepping-stone for John's whole career.

So telling Alice was out, and asking Professor Woodward's advice before reading the letters was also rejected after a little more thought. It would probably have to come to that in the end, because after all he was John's mentor and director of studies, but it would be more in accordance with Lady Heron's wishes to keep it within the family for the time being. And since there were no other members of the household except Jimmy, whom John scarcely knew, and the conspirators themselves, and the cat, it boiled down to making up his own mind and finally doing what he had known in his heart from the first that he was going to do, and what Lady Heron must have known perfectly well that he would do in spite of giving his promise not to.

He picked up some envelopes at random and began to read, devouring the letters at a far greater speed than Letty had done, although like Letty before him, he lost all sense of time and place as he read.

"Good God!" he cried aloud again and again. "How amazing!"

And then a little later: "Poor girl. Hell hath no fury . . ."

For if Emily's passion was such that it seemed to scald
the paper on which it was written, the rapid cooling-off of
her lover's was almost equally plain to the unprejudiced
reader. It was not simply that his people considered her
Bohemian background to be unsuitable for an alliance with
a Heron; it was that Roderick himself was tired of her
intensity and her possessiveness. Trying to keep their affair
secret could only have added to the strain. And at the end it
was obvious that Emily believed herself to be pregnant—or
had at any rate told him so. There was no mention of this in
the report of the inquest, but of course in such a society and
in such an era, that fact would have been suppressed.

Like Letty before him, John found himself coming to the
inevitable conclusion. "So Roderick was there," he said
very slowly out loud, thinking as he spoke. "He actually
met Emily—on Boar's Hill—by appointment at her urgent
request—on the day when she died."

The information was contained in a letter from Emily to
Lady Heron herself. It was in a plain white envelope and it
bore no address or superscription, only the date—the
twentieth of April. It was the most astonishing letter of the
lot—an extraordinary mixture of rage and jealousy, of love
and despair.

"I want you to know," it began, "that he cares nothing
for you, that he loves only me, me, me! Your marriage will
be a mockery, you will suffer for it all your life. Look at
these letters that I have written to him and those he has
written to me! Can you deny that it is I who should be his
wife? You have no claim. Are you not ashamed to be bound
to a man who loves another?"

After carrying on in this strain for some time the writer
changed her tune.

"I am meeting him tomorrow afternoon," she wrote, "at
the top of Boar's Hill at three o'clock, where we have so

often stood and gazed at the dreaming spires of Oxford together. I have something of great importance to tell him that will surely make him change his mind. And yet I am afraid."

After a few more strong hints about what that "something" was, the writer concluded with some most intriguing sentences:

"I send you these letters in case I do not succeed. Publish them if you wish. Or marry him if you dare, knowing that he is a—no, I cannot write it, my pen itself rebels against the dreadful word. But if in spite of all my warnings you join your fate with his, then even in the midst of this my greatest trial, my last bid for life and joy, I can still find it in my heart to pity you."

"Good God," said John yet again as he sat staring at the sprawling handwriting. "History repeats itself. Emily feared he might kill her and called on Isabella to take revenge. But Isabella didn't take it, and now, in mortal fear herself, she calls on me."

In a daze he gathered the letters together. He had not the slightest idea what he was going to do. He didn't even know where he could put them for safe-keeping. He was just beginning to turn his mind to this problem when to his horror he heard his landlady's step on the basement stairs.

"Coo-ee! Are you in, John?"

"Hullo, Mrs. Willey," he said, meeting her at the door. Not another soul must enter this room until he had hidden the letters; that much he was sure of.

She was puffing a little and looked rather upset.

"Oh, John, I'm terribly sorry to disturb your studies, but I wondered if you could spare me a few minutes."

"Is it the car again?" he asked, his heart sinking.

"I'm afraid so. It suddenly faded out, just like that, round the corner in Walton Street. Luckily it's quite near to the pavement, but I can't leave it there too long or the police will be after me."

"I'll come in a minute," said John, hoping that she would take the hint and go upstairs ahead of him. But she leaned against the door-post, alternately gasping for breath and thanking him. He went back into the room. At least the bed was round the corner, out of sight of the door. He picked up a paper bag with the name of the local grocer on it and thrust the letters into it. It was the best he could do on the spur of the moment. To start cramming things into drawers would attract Mrs. Willey's attention; but to any casual observer the bag would look as if it contained groceries. In any case, he comforted himself as they made their way to the stranded car, no one but Graham was likely to come into the house, and he was a sober, sensible sort of person who minded his own business and was kindly disposed towards John.

All the same the delay was sickening. It was well past seven now and the best part of an hour had elapsed since he had rushed away from Blenheim Close. They could scarcely have guessed the real reason for his unconventional exit, but they would think it very rude, at the least. After all, he had been invited to dinner, and the last thing he wanted, with these amazing revelations about the Heron family in his hands, was to be denied access to the house.

Mrs. Willey's elderly Morris Minor, which she was kind enough to lend to John occasionally and which he some-times managed to get started for her, was in a particularly recalcitrant mood this evening. It was not a jammed starter-motor and she hadn't flooded the engine. John sat there, inwardly fuming, and impotently prodding at the dash-board. He liked Mrs. Willey very much and he wanted to help her but he couldn't think what else to do. She waited patiently, her plump kindly face watching him with concern, but also with an innocent confidence in his mechanical genius.

"I'm awfully sorry," said John at last, "but I don't know what's the matter with it. I think you'd better go home and phone the A.A. I'll just try once more."

Mrs. Willey got out and walked off obediently. John applied himself to the ignition again. He was exceedingly anxious about the letters and about getting in touch with Blenheim Close, but he also loathed being beaten by anything. To his great relief the engine fired. He drove off at once, before it should change its mind, and made a couple of rounds of the block to keep it running for a while. At almost exactly the same spot where he had found the car broken down, the engine faded out again.

John swore furiously, banged on the wheel and kicked at the pedals with frustration. Then he tore out the ignition key and got out of the car. This was enough. Mrs. Willey would just have to wait for the A.A. He strode round the corner into Walton Terrace and stopped short at a little distance from the house. Who was that standing on the front doorstep with Mrs. Willey? Surely not Alice come round to see what had become of him? His heart leapt for a moment, only to sink rapidly again. Of course it wasn't Alice; she would never wear a hat and coat of such a peculiarly revolting shade of pink.

The sinking feeling increased when he saw who Mrs. Willey's companion was. He had not the slightest desire to talk to Letty at this moment and he still did not know whether he was supposed to call her Letty or Miss Mann.

"Ah, here's the truant," she cried with frightful archness as he approached. "Here's the knight-errant of the Queen's Highway. I expect he'll be forgiven, don't you, when they hear the reason for his delay?"

"My dear John," said his landlady in great distress, "why on earth didn't you tell me that Sir Roderick Heron was expecting you to dinner? I'd never have dreamed of troubling you about the car. Oh dear, I do so hope he will understand and will not think it dreadfully rude. Fancy him sending Miss Mann round to remind you!"

Mrs. Willey dearly loved a title and Letty had obviously been making the most of it. John, too, found it hard to credit that Sir Roderick had sent Letty in person to fetch him; unless—and the thought sent a little shiver of apprehension through him— the old man suspected that Lady Heron had given him something of vital importance and was going to put John through some sort of third degree. But there was no help for it, he would have to go, only he could not face the ten minutes' walk with Letty at his side.

"I'm all mucky from the car," he said. "I'll have to wash first. You go ahead and tell them I won't be long."

He ran down the area steps, hastily cleaned himself up in the kitchen, and then went into the front room. The letters would just have to go in the table drawer for the time being; there wasn't time now to think up a better hiding-place for them. He went straight over to the bed, on which he had left the brown paper bag. He thumped it all over and then he bashed at the shabby armchairs and the table and the bookcase and the cupboard and every other bit of furniture in the room. He even crawled about on the threadbare carpet and banged around the kitchen and the passage before at last his mind consented to accept the evidence of his eyes.

The brown paper bag with its explosive contents was simply not there, and unless Mrs. Willey had been down again and seen the grocer's name and picked it up thinking it was her own shopping, which was unlikely in the extreme, there was only one person who could have taken it.

John shot up the area steps again to see Letty Mann disappearing round the corner into the main road and to be assailed by a great flood of apologies from his landlady.

7

"It's all right," said John wearily. "It doesn't matter."

But Mrs. Willey had to explain all over again.

"The phone's playing up and I had ever such trouble getting through, and when I got the A.A. at last the front-door bell rang, and I couldn't bear to lose them so I told them to hang on, and I rushed to the door and saw this lady and said, 'Excuse me, I'm on the phone, I won't be a moment,' and she said, 'Well, actually it was Mr. John Broome I wanted,' so I said, 'He's in the basement but he's not there because he's trying to start my car,' and then I simply dared not keep the A.A. man waiting any longer, so I rushed back to the phone and they took absolutely ages to get down the particulars and when at last I'd finished I turned and I couldn't see the lady and I thought she'd gone without my noticing and I felt terribly discourteous, and then she came up the basement stairs and said, 'You're quite right, Mr. Broome isn't there,' and then we got talking and she told me who she was and how Alice was worried about where you were—you don't mind me calling her Alice, do you, she's such a sweet girl—and oh dear I do so hope Sir Roderick isn't angry with you for being so late. I do so hope everything will be all right, John."

"It will be all right," said John, and made his escape.

It was no good blaming Mrs. Willey. She was only the innocent instrument of that scheming Letty, who must have known all along about those letters and had guessed that Lady Heron had given them to him. She had devised a bold and simple plan to get them back and good luck had been on her side in the shape of Mrs. Willey's tottery old Morris. And what now, wondered John as he raced along. How and when would Letty try to play her ace of trumps? Would she try right away to blackmail Sir Roderick into promising to marry her? Or wait until Lady Heron had been disposed of? And did she realize what a dangerous game she was playing, and if by some miracle of good luck she succeeded, could she really marry the old man believing him to be a murderer? Well, she would not be the first woman to have done so, thought John as he arrived at Blenheim Close; not if he had read Emily's letters aright.

He walked up the path to the house, a dim ragged outline now with its turrets and gables against the darkening sky, with very different feelings from those with which he had first approached it. It had been a fascinating Victorian relic to him then; but now it seemed to him more like the home of some Gothic horror story. It was terrifying indeed, but not in the sense in which Alice had used the word.

Alice! He had only time to wonder what part Alice was playing in all this and whether she had any suspicions at all about the basis of her uncle and aunt's marriage, when the door was opened to him. Letty had presumably only that moment arrived, for she was still wearing the pink hat and coat. The handles of her big black handbag hung over her arm.

"You've got a heavy load there," said John, looking at it. "Shall I relieve you of it?"

She flushed an ugly red and clasped the bag to her. "I'll tell them you're here," she said.

They stared at each other. The house was deathly quiet. For a wild moment John thought of tackling her, putting a hand over her mouth, grabbing the bag, and once again beating an unceremonious retreat with the loot. He was saved from this lunacy by the appearance of Alice in the drawing-room door. Voices from the television set were audible in the room behind her.

"Who's that at the door, Letty?" she asked listlessly. And then catching sight of the pink hat and coat: "Oh—have you been out? I thought you were in the kitchen washing up the dinner things."

There was a casual arrogance in Alice's voice and manner that John had never been conscious of in her before. Yet another unpleasant suspicion entered his mind, and it was confirmed by Alice's next words.

"Hullo, John," she said. It was the most off-hand of greetings. "I didn't expect to see you here again this evening."

He was struck speechless, and Letty hastened to explain.

"I knew you and your uncle were worrying about his rushing off like that," she said to Alice, "so I thought as soon as we'd finished eating I'd go and see what he was up to."

Then I wasn't sent for, thought John, with a little wriggle of shame at his own vanity for momentarily believing it possible; that was just part of Letty's plot.

"I said to myself," continued Letty, "that boy's got something to hide, I said. Only someone with a very guilty conscience would dash away like that after being made so welcome in this house."

But this time she had overreached herself. "Oh, don't be so silly, Letty," said Alice irritably. "John hasn't been stealing the silver."

"Not the silver, maybe," retorted Letty, "but he'd got something stuffed in his pockets when he came downstairs. I saw it plain as plain."

You bitch, said John to himself; I'll make you suffer for this if it's the last thing I do in this world.

"It's perfectly true," he said, turning to Alice. "I did have something in my pockets. Your aunt had a couple of little packets she wanted sent in the last post today and I only just caught it. I don't know what they were and I don't know why she asked me, and I'd have come straight back after posting them, but I saw Mrs. Willey's car broken down in the road and you know what follows that."

That's one in the eye for you, madam, he added, mentally addressing Letty. It would be very gratifying to make her open up her handbag and reveal the letters and her own duplicity, right there in front of Alice, but it was out of the question and both he and Letty knew it. They were at the moment hostile, unwilling allies. If Alice got a sight of those letters that would be an end of all their hopes and aims. They would sink together.

"I see," said Alice in slightly less unfriendly tones. "What a funny thing for Auntie to do. Why did she ask you to do it?"

John began to revive a little. It looked as if she was at any rate going to appear to believe his story, and after all, he recollected, he had in fact called out as he rushed from the house that he was going to post something for Lady Heron. Perhaps there was hope for him with Alice yet. He was meditating his next move, and Letty too was exclaiming over the strange behaviour of Lady Heron, when another voice was added to those of the three standing in the hall.

"What on earth is all this row about? I'm trying to draft an important letter to my solicitor and I can't hear myself think."

Sir Roderick was standing in the door of his den, in a great fury, glaring indiscriminately at each one of them in turn, a steely glitter in his eye.

"Is there insufficient accommodation in this house that you have to do your silly chattering right outside my door?" he bellowed.

John tried to shrink into the shadows at the foot of the stairs; Letty visibly trembled, and even Alice seemed shaken.

"Please, Uncle," she begged, "don't shout so. You'll wake Auntie. We won't disturb you any more. We'll go into the drawing-room."

"You, sir," said Sir Roderick, lowering his voice a trifle and appearing to catch sight of John for the first time. "You here again?"

"He was helping an old lady to get her car going," said Alice quickly before John had time to think of a suitable reply. "That's why he didn't come back in time for dinner."

"A very worthy excuse," said Sir Roderick, "if you choose to believe it."

This time it was Alice's turn to flush. "I do believe it," she said. "It was his landlady. John is very kind to her."

Sir Roderick stared in amazement. He turned his head from Alice to John and then back to Alice again, and his lip curled in the way that John had come to know so well.

"Your—er—friend seems to have rather a way with old ladies," he said at last. "It remains to be seen whether he is as successful at getting off with a young one." He stepped back into the doorway of his room and his eye fell upon

Letty. "And what d'you think you are doing here," he asked, "all dressed up like a dog's dinner? I should like some strong coffee and a brandy, and I should also be grateful if I may be allowed a little peace and quiet in my own house."

The door of the room closed noisily behind him. The three people standing in the hall blinked and shook themselves and went their several ways without another word, Letty to the kitchen, Alice and John into the drawing-room, where she switched off the television and offered him a drink.

"My God, I needed that," he said, gulping down the whisky.

She smiled faintly. "I did warn you about him, John."

"I know you did, but it's quite another thing to experience it."

She sat down and he ventured to do the same. She seemed to be thawing a little, but he was afraid of making a premature advance. She had stood up for him against her uncle, and that was a good sign, but he still felt that there was something gravely wrong between them, and it was not just that she was offended because he had rushed away from the house without stopping to speak to her. Alice would never hold a grievance about a little thing like that. Unconsciously imitating Sir Roderick's technique, he waited for her to make the first move.

"If only you could have controlled yourself, John," she said sadly. "I told you that he might try and make you lose your temper."

"But I didn't," burst out John, and then took a very deep breath and a very firm grip upon himself indeed. "What did your uncle tell you about our interview?" he asked quietly.

"He said how interesting your studies sounded, and how he thought you seemed to be making a very good job of it and that you ought to go far in your career. I told you I thought you had made a good impression. It's such a pity that you didn't take my advice and count ten before replying when he started getting under your skin." There was a catch in her voice and John believed there were tears in her eyes. "I know he's infuriating," she went on, "but he's been bossing people about all his life and he's an old man now and you can't expect him to change. You just have to put up with him as he is."

John looked at her fair head, turned away from him now and bent low over the arm of her chair. His heart went out to her but he dared not move and scarcely dared to speak.

"What did he say?" he repeated very softly.

"He said you'd been very disrespectful," she said, still keeping her face averted and tracing with her finger the pattern of the crimson upholstery on the arm of the chair. "He said he was really afraid at one moment that you were going to strike him and he was glad that Jimmy was within call, and when I asked Jimmy about it he said just the same."

"And you believe this?" said John, still speaking very calmly and quietly. "You really believe me capable of threatening an old man, your nearest relative?"

"I don't know." She looked round at him then, her grey eyes moist and very troubled, her fine, slightly haughty features wrinkled up with distress. "I don't know what to think, except that I know you can be very impulsive and that Uncle Rod doesn't tell lies."

Doesn't tell lies, repeated John to himself, as he gazed unhappily back at her. The outrageous audacity of the thing took away his breath. Deprived of the chance to show John up to Alice as an impotent, fumbling young fool, Sir Roderick had turned his forces round to attack from the opposite direction and had presented John as a potentially violent young man, with a lot of good in him no doubt, but one about whom Alice ought to think very seriously indeed if she didn't want to make her poor old uncle suffer. The seeds of doubt had been very skilfully sown in her mind, accompanied by a praise of John himself that might just possibly be sincere in its way.

He felt utterly at a loss. There was nothing one could do against tactics like this. His only weapon—a very powerful two-edged sword—was at this moment still reposing in Letty's handbag, or in whatever other temporary hiding-place she had found for it. But even if he could present the evidence to Alice and make her believe it and say to her in effect: Look here, this dear old uncle of yours whom one has to humour in his funny little ways is a ruthless liar and schemer and a cold-blooded murderer, what good would that do? She would fly to his defence, as she had flown to John's just now, ever taking the part of the threatened party. It would be some sort of victory over Sir Roderick, he supposed, but the taste of it would be very bitter in his mouth.

They stared at each other in silent unhappiness and doubt. The door opened and Letty entered carrying a tray.

"I've made you some sandwiches and coffee," she said to John, simpering at him, "as you missed your dinner."

"Thank you, Letty," said Alice absently. "It's very good of you to think of it."

"Thank you," said John, unable to keep the gruffness out of his voice. He picked up one of the sandwiches and peered inside it, hardly aware that he was doing so.

"It's perfectly good ham," said Letty. "There's no poison in it if that's what you're worried about."

John hurriedly apologized and took a large bite at the sandwich.

"I think I'll go to bed if you don't need anything more,"

said Letty to Alice. "I'm a little tired after all this activity today. Besides—" and her eye met John's—"I've a nice little thriller of Victorian times that I'm right in the middle of at the moment."

John ignored this, but Alice gave a nervous little laugh. "Letty loves thrillers," she said. "So do Uncle and Auntie. I'm afraid the literary tastes of this household are not quite up to your standards, John. Except for the nurse. She's brought *War and Peace* to read on night duty."

When Letty had left the room John said: "I wasn't suspecting her, you know. I only wanted to see what was in the sandwich."

"Yes, I know," said Alice. "Don't take any notice of her. She's been quite intolerable all evening. I suppose it was rather awful having Auntie accuse her like that and then being turned out of the room and having the nurse put in charge of preparing food for Auntie."

John noted this last fact with relief but said nothing out loud. He still didn't know quite how he stood with Alice. "What did the doctor say?" he asked, feeling that this question was safe enough, and really wanting to know the answer.

"It's a severe attack of gastroenteritis," Alice replied. "She's had it before, and she's been having it on and off the last couple of weeks. Dr. Lethbridge always does her good. She started on about someone trying to poison her and he said she didn't need any poisoners around when she was quite capable of doing the job herself by eating such unsuitable things on a weak stomach. He actually got a laugh out of her. She was ever so much better after you had gone, John."

I dare say she was, he thought, and it wasn't only because of the doctor's merry quips. But again he kept this thought to himself. To remain perfectly calm and noncommittal and let Alice be the first to give way to her feelings was his best course now, and this time he deliberately put into practice the painful lesson that he had learnt from Alice's uncle. As she talked on he could see she was at first a little surprised, and then distinctly provoked, by his seeming placidity.

"You're very silent, John," she said at last.

He smiled at her affectionately but made no response.

"Damn you, what are you playing at?" she demanded angrily.

"I'll give you one guess," he replied.

She threw a cushion at him and he fielded it and put it aside. The next moment she was on his knee and they were entwined together. It was thus that Sir Roderick found them when he came into the room a few minutes later. He seemed to have recovered his normal poise, or else he had decided once more to change his tactics, for he gave a loud cough, which caused them to spring apart, and then he said heartily: "Well, well. I seem to have chosen a bad moment. All I wanted, Alice, was to say that I've now drafted that letter and shall ask you to type it for me in the morning. I'm going to turn in early, as it's been a somewhat tiring day."

John got to his feet. With Alice's kisses warm on his lips he was feeling brave again. "I'm going now, sir," he said. "I'm very sorry if I've added to your inconveniences today."

Sir Roderick gave his expansive wave of the arm. "Not at all, my dear chap. It's been a pleasure to get to know you. Don't feel obliged to leave just yet. Stay and—er—" He paused significantly. "Enjoy yourself. Make yourself at home."

Again the hospitable gesture and the warmth in the deep voice, but John eyed him warily as he made a polite reply. This tiger was never so dangerous as when there was a broad smile on his face.

Sir Roderick paused at the door. "You'll lock up, will you, my love?" he said to Alice.

"Yes, Uncle."

Alice looked very embarrassed and grateful not to be scolded, as if she were a small girl being treated indulgently after being caught playing with her mother's cosmetics. John could see her mind working, could see it swinging round again already to Sir Roderick's side.

"And you'll call Quizzy, won't you, if he isn't in before you go to bed?"

"Yes, dear Uncle Rod. I promise I will."

"You know how we do it?"

"Yes, dear Uncle."

He inclined his head for her to kiss him and then left the room.

"I'm going home now, all the same," said John. "It's getting late and I think we're all tired."

He felt awkward now, alone with Alice. Sir Roderick's florid permissiveness had somehow cast a blight over their embrace. Alice seemed to feel it too, for she made no protest.

"How do you call Quizzy?" asked John, not merely out of idle curiosity, as they moved to the door. He had been aware of something missing in the house during the evening—a little soft furry presence that cheered up the whole place, miraculously easing tensions and turning this grim house of plots and fears and suspicions into something like a home again. "I'd like to see him again before I go," he added.

"I'll show you," said Alice.

She led the way to the kitchen, opened a cupboard and took out an old cardboard box containing what looked to John at first like a few bits of old iron. Then he recognized what it was.

"Good Lord," he cried. "An old mincing machine. My grandmother had one but I didn't know anyone ever used them nowadays if they could afford an electric mixer."

"Letty does occasionally," replied Alice. "She says it gives a better result for some dishes, but I rather suspect it's a bit of masochism on her part. Anyway, it's useful for calling Quizzy." She took the pieces out of the box. "We needn't bother to fix it to the table. As long as we can turn the handle."

John held the antique mincer, diverted but at the same time a little anxious. He could not help fearing that the various intrigues that were taking place in the household were going to claim some victim sooner or later, and he felt that he would be very glad indeed to see Quizzy.

"Letty discovered it by accident," explained Alice, "when she was putting some cold turkey through the mincer for a pie and Quizzy suddenly appeared from nowhere and demanded some. And ever since then it's worked like a charm—as long as he's not too far away to hear the squeaking handle. Go and open the back door and you'll see."

They worked away for several minutes and then John said: "Does he usually take all this time to react?"

Alice shook her head. "He must have wandered right down the road."

John was conscious of a strong sense of apprehension, but he did not mention it to Alice. His mind went back to the little comedy that had been played out between Sir Roderick and the gardener about the weedkiller, and to Jimmy's muttered remark, out of earshot of Sir Roderick: "What's the guv'nor up to now? He knows the cat never touches it." That remark seemed to John one of the few completely honest things he had heard said in this house. He could think of a number of things that the guv'nor, or Letty if she was working so far in conjunction with him, might be up to. They could be trying out on the cat whether the taste of the poisonous powder was noticeable if concealed in chicken curry, for example, with a view to its eventual introduction into a human stomach. And Alice herself, after some further unsuccessful operations, unwittingly suggested another possibility.

"I do hope nothing's happened to him," she said, looking almost as worried as John was now feeling. "I don't know how we can break it to Auntie if Quizzy were to go missing. The doctor says she mustn't have any shock or any great distress if it can possibly be avoided. I really do believe it could kill her."

In theory, thought John, it sounded rather absurd to suggest that the disappearance or death of her pet cat could also mean the death of a very sick and feeble old lady, but in the present circumstances it didn't seem absurd at all; on the contrary, it was sinister and peculiarly unpleasant.

"I don't think there is much point in going on with this," he said, taking the mincer from Alice's hands. "I think we had better go and look for him in the garden. As a matter of fact I saw him near the laburnum tree by the front gate when I went to post those packets for Auntie Belle."

"But that was hours ago," cried Alice. "He won't still be there now."

"I've got a feeling that he may be," said John.

— 8 —

They searched by the light of the street-lamp near the front
gate. Or rather, John searched while Alice stood in tense
silence. Next to the laburnum there grew a lilac bush whose
lowest branches brushed the ground. It was while pushing
these aside that John felt the soft fur. He ran his hand along
it; the sickness at heart mounted to acute nausea accompanied by grief as if he had lost a friend. After a moment or
two he said softly: "I've found him. And I'm afraid he's
dead."

He heard Alice give a little gasp before she spoke. "Are
you sure? Perhaps he's only asleep. Or had a heart attack.
He's a very old cat, you know, although he's so active."

"He's dead, I'm afraid," said John after investigating
further. "There's no doubt about it. There's no breathing at
all."

Alice gasped again and then said, with some firmness:
"Laburnum is poisonous, isn't it?"

"I believe so," replied John with a fresh sinking feeling, but this time it was for a different reason.

"Then that explains it," said Alice more firmly and with a note of relief in her voice. "He must have eaten some of the seeds."

"Possibly," said John, "although the seeds are hardly forming yet, and presumably he hasn't touched them in previous years. Anyway, we shall soon find out."

"Find out? How?" Alice's voice was unpleasantly shrill.

"Get an autopsy done."

"But who would do it?" Alice sounded near hysteria. "You don't have to notify the police over the death of a cat."

So she does know something, thought John; she was not entirely a little innocent. And she was terrified of anyone finding out what had killed the cat. She wouldn't worry if she thought it was anyone else but she would lie to the death to defend her uncle.

The pendulum of Alice's loyalty and love, which had been swinging violently about all day and indeed for some weeks past, appeared now to John to move right over to the side of the old man and to remain there, a dead weight, sounding the death knell of all his dearest hopes. He had regained quite a lot of ground since his return to the house, he believed, and he believed he could win back even more, given half a chance. The call of youth to youth was very strong. But he would have to give in now and back up any story that Alice liked to suggest to account for the death of the cat. And he couldn't do it. There was not even a second's temptation to do so. Pain and anger rose up and exploded within him as he thought of the lively inquisitive little creature who had brightened up the whole household, who lapped up cream in a disdainful manner but who must have guzzled down the fatal dish so greedily. And who, above all, had provided the one little bit of loving contact in a sick old woman's life.

It was absolutely beastly, and it was damned well not going to be hushed up; it was going to be thoroughly investigated, whoever got hurt in the process.

"Could you find me a big cardboard box or some other container?" he said. "I don't want to have to carry him all the way home like this."

"But, John . . ." She sounded outraged now. There was that touch of arrogance in her voice that he had noticed for the first time that evening when she had greeted him so coolly. "There is absolutely no need whatever for you to do anything about it," she went on. "We can put a piece of old blanket over him now and Jimmy will attend to it all in the morning."

"He bloody well won't," said John grimly. "Over my dead body, that is. I'm taking this cat off now and I'm going to find out what killed him. So will you kindly go and fetch me that box?"

There was a silence. They faced each other, standing a few feet apart, in a mixture of deep shadow and the faint light that came from the street-lamp.

"All right," said Alice at last. "There's one in the garden shed, I think."

John stood breathing heavily after she had gone. He had won some sort of a victory, he supposed, but it was not the sort that he ever wished to win again. He was shaken through and through with fury and distress; all his deepest instincts were outraged. And behind it all was a dim vision of a miserable future—a future without Alice, who had come to mean everything to him, and without whom all effort would be meaningless, all success a mockery, all experience stale.

He bent down and ran his hand over the fur on the limp little body of the cat.

"Oh, Quizzy, Quizzy," he whispered. "Why did you have to be so greedy, you silly little devil? Look what you've gone and done to us all!"

Alice returned with a large cardboard box and handed it to John without a word. He placed the corpse in it and folded over the flaps so that it could not be seen. Then he stood by the open gate holding his pitiful burden under one arm. Neither of them had yet spoken, but surely they would at least have to say good night. Alice made a little movement towards him, catching at his free arm.

He put the box down on the ground and caught her to him. She broke down at last and he could feel her convulsive sobbing.

"Ssh. Ssh. It will all come right in the end." He soothed her with meaningless phrases.

"I can't bear you to think," she said at last, "that I don't care about Quizzy. I—I—I— " There was another burst of tears. "I was terribly fond of him," she went on. "We grew up together, Quizzy and I. He was nearly fourteen. And he was wonderfully healthy but he couldn't have lasted much longer. He'd have got too feeble to go on his jaunts and he'd simply have hated that. So he hasn't really lost so very much, you see."

She broke off to weep again.

"I suppose not," said John wearily. He was feeling not far off tears himself. Alice's attempts at self-justification seemed to him pitiable but at the same time somewhat nauseating. That Quizzy had been an old cat was not the point at all. But there was no sense in rubbing salt into her sore conscience and increasing her own wretchedness, for now that the first shock was receding he could appreciate that she would have a tough time ahead of her.

"How are you going to tell Auntie Belle?" he asked.

"I think," she said, giving a big gulp and brushing a hand over her eyes, "that I'll get the nurse to forbid animals in the sickroom. That will save us a day, and perhaps the next day she'll be stronger and more able to bear it."

John approved of the idea. It was a little comfort to him to know that she could still feel for her aunt's grief, even with the great worry that was on her mind. To lose Alice herself might just be borne, provided he could still love and respect her.

He did not ask her what she was going to say to her uncle; it was better that the old man's name should not be mentioned between them. He kissed her again, begged her to try and get some rest, and asked her to ring him at Mrs. Willey's if she had anything to tell him the following morning.

And then for the second time that day John found himself going away from Number Eleven Blenheim Close bearing an embarrassing burden. The only consolation was that this time he knew exactly what it was and what he was going to do about it.

When he got back to Walton Terrace he glanced up to see whether there was light shining behind the curtains of the front room on the first floor. Good, he said to himself: Graham poring over his formulae as usual. He deposited his burden in the basement and crept quietly upstairs to make his request. Mrs. Willey, exhausted no doubt by her motoring activities, had gone to bed.

Graham Price was a good-natured, hard-working chemistry student, who was very happy to oblige a friend by making use of his access to the University laboratories, and who was blessedly tactful and asked no awkward questions.

"I think I can fix it," he said cheerfully when John had

explained what he wanted. "It'll make quite a change for me."

"Tomorrow morning? So that I know the answer by lunch-time?"

"Well, I don't know how full a report," began Graham more doubtfully.

"No report at all," John assured him. "Don't go to any more trouble than is necessary. If I could just have the gist of it in layman's terms, as if you were an expert witness explaining to the dimmest member of the jury. Could you phone me here at lunch-time, do you think?"

Graham thought he might manage to have some news by then.

"If I sound a bit off-hand on the phone," said John, "you'll know that Mrs. Willey is hovering. I'd rather she didn't know about this if you don't mind. And if you could come and remove the box without her seeing. She might be upset, you see, thinking of her own cat."

"If we disembowelled that one it would be found to have died of a surfeit of cream cakes," said Graham. "If anyone asks at the lab, by the way, I'll just say I'm doing it for a friend, shall I? They can think it's a neurotic old lady who suspects the neighbours of having poisoned her cat."

"Yes, you say that," said John.

He thanked Graham warmly and padded downstairs to the basement. There he flung off his clothes and fell into bed, more exhausted in mind than on the last day of his Finals, and more exhausted in body than after the most strenuous of his cross-country runs. His last waking thought was that instead of a brown paper bag containing valuable letters, he now had a brown cardboard box containing the worthless corpse of a much-loved cat. The two came together in his sleep and produced the weirdest of dreams.

When Graham collected the box early next morning he

still asked no questions but his eyes surveyed John with some concern through thick lenses.

"I'll ring as soon as I can," he promised.

"Thanks. I shan't be going out. I'm going to have a blitz on all the dope I've collected on my poet."

Graham gave a little cough and said sententiously: "All work and no play . . . Seriously, John, why don't you give it a miss this morning and go for a long walk or have a game of squash or something? It'd do you good."

"Look who's talking. When did you last neglect your studies?"

"Oh well, it's different with scientists. We have to plod slowly away at the pace our experiments are going. We're not knocked out by waves of inspiration like you literary johnnies."

"I wish a wave of inspiration would come and hit me now," said John as he pushed Graham out of the room.

"Anyway, let Mrs. W. come and cook you some breakfast," was the latter's parting shot.

John decided to take this very sound piece of advice. It salved Mrs. Willey's conscience for the difficulties she had led John into, although of course she was only aware of the half of them, and it soothed his troubled mind to listen to her homely chatter about simple familiar things. This was his rightful place in the world, he thought; a shabby basement flat and the widow of a primary schoolteacher sitting with him at the Formica-topped kitchen table, pouring strong tea into a big blue and white striped mug.

"Are the Herons very grand?" she asked presently.

John described their drawing-room for her and she listened with great eagerness and then told him about an occasion when she and her husband had been invited to a gathering at some stately home.

"What did you have for dinner?" she asked next.

He invented a convincing menu, and in answer to further enquiries explained that Lady Heron was an invalid, that Sir Roderick was a fine old chap and amazingly friendly, and that Miss Mann seemed to live as one of the family as far as he could see. Mrs Willey lapped it all up and John thought wryly that he had in fact been describing the household exactly as it must appear to all but the most privileged insiders.

When Mrs. Willey had gone out shopping he made a telephone call to his professor. This was the morning when the group of research students met to report progress and exchange ideas, the day on which John was triumphantly to have reported on the interview with somebody who had actually known his poet.

"I'm afraid I shan't be coming to the meeting," he said when Professor Woodward came on to the line.

"I am sorry to hear that," said the Professor rather coolly, and waited in silence for John to give a reason.

"I—well, as a matter of fact I've run into a bit of a snag," said John. Might as well start breaking the news at once. He was going to have to tell Sam Woodward sooner or later that his researches into Emily Witherington's life and work would either have to be very drastically revised or come to an end altogether.

"Really? What sort of a snag?" The voice at the other end of the line was warmer now. "Anything I can do to help?"

"I can't very well explain it on the phone. I've gone and uncovered something that I don't think ought to go into the book and I'd be grateful for your advice."

"Aha. Turned up a bit of dirt, eh?" The voice was positively genial now. "That's one of the occupational hazards of the biographer. You'll have to get used to that sort of problem, my lad. All right then. Give this morning a miss and come up to my place this evening. The girls will be home then and pleased to see you."

Professor Woodward had two witty and good-natured daughters of marriageable age. In his present hypersensitive condition, when every little remark seemed weighed down with hidden meanings, John found himself wondering whether this was the Professor's tactful way of warning him that there was no point in trying for Alice. He accepted the invitation and was about to ring off when Professor Woodward said: "Bit of a scandal, eh? Not to do with the Herons by any chance?"

"Well, yes, it is," admitted John.

"Phew! Have to go carefully there. You're quite right to tell me. Which one of them? Nothing to do with Alice, I trust?

"No, not Alice," said John, but the moment he had spoken all sorts of crazy ideas began to come into his mind. Perhaps it would turn out to do with Alice after all. Perhaps at some time Emily had actually had a child. Perhaps that child had in turn had a daughter who would be Alice's age now. What a fascinating thought, that Alice could actually be Emily Witherington's grandchild! But it was out of the question; she was descended from distinguished army officers who had married suitable consorts, and he really would have to rein in his imagination or it would get him into trouble.

Professor Woodward was talking again. "Good. I wouldn't want any breath of scandal ever to touch our Alice. Lady Heron perhaps? She was a Molyneux, you know. Daughter of the *Foundations of Perception* Molyneux, and a bit of a bluestocking in her own right too, though hardly a beauty. Must've been the talk of the town when she landed the most eligible bachelor of that generation."

"Look," said John, wondering why he had never noticed before what a frightful gossip Sam Woodward was. "Look—er—Sam." He cleared his throat. He never really felt comfortable using the Professor's Christian name, but such mateyness was becoming the rule of the day in progressive circles and you made yourself into an outsider if you didn't conform. "It's to do with the other member of the family and I honestly don't think I'd better say any more on the phone."

"The old 'un himself? Well, well. Quite a lad in his day, no doubt."

"It's not that. It's something much worse," said John in despair. This produced another interested whistle, but at least it did bring the conversation to an end, and John hung up the receiver and placed the tuppence for the call in the box provided with the feeling that he had at least shifted a little of the burden from his own shoulders. Sam Woodward might enjoy a bit of gossip, but he was discreet enough when it came to anything that really mattered and his advice was always sound. It would be an enormous relief to tell him the whole story, and by then he would have heard from Graham about the cat, and perhaps even from Alice. He was longing to know how things were going in Blenheim Close, but felt it safest from all points of view to let Alice herself make the first move.

Meanwhile there was the melancholy task of trying to salvage some of the work he had put in on Emily. The biographical stuff would have to be completely changed, except for the first chapter which gave a short account of her childhood and her parents' background and life style. He felt quite sickened as he glanced through the paragraphs he had written containing speculations as to the identity of the unknown lover who was the subject of "Arbour of Roses" and so many of her poems. How foolish it all looked now, all these silly little bits of conjecture and so-called "evidence," showing that it could possibly have been this man or that who was known to have played some sort of a part in her life! And not the slightest hint anywhere of who the man really was. How Sir Roderick must have chuckled to himself when he made those remarks about the veracity of his own memories compared with the assumptions made by the hopeful young literary historian! The very thought of that interview made John blush all over.

He picked up Emily's last volume of poems and flicked through it. In the light of his present knowledge they took on an unbearable poignancy. "The Dead Willow Tree," for example, where the poet waited by the hollow stump of an old pollard willow in the chill evening air, knowing that her lover would not come. Slight overtones of "Mariana" this time—she had certainly been soaking herself in Tennyson—but it still had a quality of her very own. That putting her hand through the hole in the trunk and feeling round the prickly bark inside in the forlorn hope of finding some message there—"No kernel nestled in that shrivelled husk"—that was typical Emily Witherington. She was rather fond of depicting herself as a famished song-thrush.

Poor Emily. What a painful and sad little life. And yet after all she had succeeded in doing what every poet must long to do: she had died leaving behind her words that still sang in the mind and echoed in the heart, and that would continue to do so for as long as the language was read and as long as men and women continued to love each other. And she would probably never have written them at all if she had not known and loved her Roderick.

The morning wore on. John worked away at the chapters that he had already drafted of this book which was to make his name, striking out sentence after sentence that was completely inapplicable in the light of all he now knew.

Even the comments on the poems which he had written after
much thought and study, looked now to be hopelessly
irrelevant. The whole thing seemed to have been written
about a different woman altogether. It would do well
enough for readers who knew nothing of his heroine; it
might well be acceptable by the academic establishment as
a conscientious piece of literary research, but to him it now
rang completely untrue.

It was hopeless. All his work was wasted. In his disgust
and disappointment he flung the mutilated typescript away
with such force that it flew all over the table and over the
floor. He stared wretchedly at the tumbled sheets of paper.
They weren't even worth putting together again; the whole
thing was rubbish. His head sank forward upon his hands
and for a few minutes he remained there motionless.

And then suddenly he sat upright and banged his fist
furiously on the table. He was damned if he was going to sit
back meekly and let these sneering aristocrats ruin his
prospects and break his heart. So his book was a non-starter,
but there was another task ahead. If Alice had plumped for
her uncle and the honour of the family, then so be it. At
least that would leave John free to fight with no holds
barred. And at least he would be doing as Lady Heron had
wished, and as she must doubly wish now if her husband
really was responsible for the death of her cat.

He pushed the typescript pages aside and took out from
his files all the papers that related to Emily's death. Never
mind about academic standards now; this was a detective
job. With the help of the glaring spotlight that the reading of
Emily's letters had thrown upon the case, surely it would be
possible to find some real hard evidence of the old man's
guilt? No mention of a Heron anywhere in the reports, of
course; there wouldn't be. But wait a minute, here was a

familiar name. Molyneux. He had heard it only a short while ago. She was daughter of the *Foundations of Perception* Molyneux, Professor Woodward had said. Daughter of the eminent philosopher who had dominated the University's thought for a decade. Her father is a noted scholar, Emily had written.

Eagerly John scanned the reports of the inquest. The body had been found by a group of young people out for an afternoon stroll. Of course some of them had been called to give evidence. First of all a Captain Frederick Walsh—a very clear and efficient witness. His was the main account. Walsh? The name meant nothing to John. But the next witness, who did little more than confirm the previous account, was a girl, and her name meant a great deal. Miss I. Molyneux. The "I.M." who was mentioned in Emily's letters, the "suitable match," the rival to whom Emily had at the last sent the whole story of her love in the hope, perhaps, that Isabella herself might be moved or disgusted enough not to marry Roderick after all, and that Emily herself might win him back.

So Lady Heron had actually been among the group of youngsters who had found Emily's body. And she had known Emily was going to cycle out to Boar's Hill that afternoon because Emily herself had told her.

John hesitated with his pen poised over the sheet of paper on which he had been making brief notes of the affair. He ought to add this bit and he didn't want to. He didn't want to think the thoughts to which the revelation might lead. Lady Heron cannot have had anything to do with it, he told himself; she would never have given me the letters and asked me to bring her husband to justice if she knew it could lead to my suspecting her of the murder herself.

No, no. He would leave that bit aside for the moment.

The job on hand was to find evidence against Sir Roderick. He began to write again, amplifying and underlining the essential points, convincing himself more and more as he wrote. The man was ruthless, heartless, cruel, and must always have been so. But so handsome and charming that the girls buzzed around him like flies.

He was dragged out of the depths of thought by the sound of a loud knocking at the area door. That must be Graham, bringing the verdict himself.

"Come in," he yelled, finishing the sentence that he was writing. "The door's not locked."

He put down his pen and turned round. A tall girl with fair hair straggling damply across her brow, and wearing a very smart raincoat that was glisteningly wet, stood hesitating in the doorway.

"Alice!" he cried, jumping up and rushing towards her. And then he caught himself up, fearful of being repulsed, of having some new hurt to bear. "I didn't know it was raining," he said idiotically.

She clutched at his hands in the trusting, appealing way that was so familiar to him.

"Help me, John, for God's sake!" she pleaded. "I don't know what to do. There's been the most frightful row I've ever known. Uncle has gone berserk and nearly murdered Letty, and now she's vanished, and he's gone off in the car with Jimmy and I don't know where. Oh, John, I'm so frightened! Please come, please come."

He caught her close and murmured soothing words. His heart was singing and he felt the strength of Samson in his arms. Alice had come to him and nothing else mattered now.

"I'll come at once," he said.

And then the telephone rang on the ground floor above, a loud bell, piercingly audible all over the house.

"Oh damn," cried John. "I'll have to answer that first."

He drew her towards a chair, said, "I won't be long," and ran. It was bound to be Graham on the phone and the call couldn't possibly have come at a worse moment.

— 9 —

When Letty Mann carried off her prize to her own room under the very nose of her defeated adversary, she experienced the most triumphant moment of her whole life. The sudden uprush of good fortune was so overwhelming that she hardly knew how to contain herself.

It had all begun with her abrupt dismissal from Lady Heron's room. She had come down to the kitchen to see Sir Roderick himself actually placing the dish with the cat's dinner down on the floor under the table.

"My dear Letty," he said, smiling very kindly as he straightened up again. "You seem to be having a somewhat trying day, so I am relieving you of this little task. I took the liberty of dipping into the curry. It seems to be going down very well with Quizzy."

The warm, appreciative voice had been like balm to Letty's aggrieved spirit. Alice had then come in, and looked rather oddly at them both, and begun to fuss around the kitchen in a way that was quite unlike her, and that seemed to irritate her uncle, because he had then asked her to go upstairs and fetch him a book that she had taken from his room. She had gone very reluctantly, but Letty had been thrilled because it was clear that Sir Roderick wanted to get rid of Alice and talk to her, Letty, alone. He had been perfectly lovely then and she had told him about Lady Heron's saying she was being poisoned, but not about the accusation of spying, which it was safer to keep to herself, as later events were to confirm.

"I don't think we use any poisonous substances in this household," Sir Roderick had then said. "Except weed-killer. I had to speak to Jimmy about that this afternoon, and take the stuff away from him. I have put it in that high cupboard, so no one could pick it up by mistake."

"Very wise," said Letty, and the most wonderfully understanding look had passed between them.

Later on, of course, he had snapped at her in the hall, but then he always did when he was in a temper, and it was probably for public consumption, because he had been charming again when she took him his coffee and brandy. It really did seem as if he was going out of his way to placate her, but whether it was to make up for Lady Heron having been so unpleasant, or whether it was because he guessed that she knew something, Letty could not decide. It would be best, perhaps, not to try to make any plan of action, but to wait on events and seize the opportunity when it arose. Just as she had done so brilliantly successfully when the young man's landlady had let her into the house.

Letty was much too excited to go to bed. She moved restlessly around the room, which was comfortable enough, but at the moment she felt herself to be so full of wonderful potentialities that it was frustrating to be enclosed in one modest apartment. Then she tried to read but could not concentrate. It all seemed so insipid in comparison with the present happenings in her own life. Finally she moved to her window, which was at the side of the house, drew aside the curtain a little, and stared out at the night.

Thus it was that she saw the figure slinking along in the shadows below, carrying something bulky. Burglars? Somehow Letty didn't think so. At any rate she was far more afraid of arousing the rest of the household than she was of attack from an intruder as she tiptoed past Sir Roderick's room and past Lady Heron's door, where a crack of light coming from underneath showed that the nurse was still reading. Half a minute was enough for her to slip silently out of the back door and round the side of the house, and the lilac bushes in front provided excellent cover for her to come close enough to hear what was said by the couple near the gate. She gathered at once that the cat had been found dead, but that didn't worry her; in fact it was a relief to know the vicious brute was out of the way. It had probably picked up some of the weedkiller that Jimmy had been told not to use, or died of a heart attack as Alice suggested.

What interested Letty was the young man's stupid and obstinate behaviour. Interfering in the family's affairs like that! This time you've dished yourself for good, my boy, she said to herself with relish. Alice was obviously furious, and so would Sir Roderick be when he heard about it, which Letty was determined he should at the first available opportunity. She did not see the two young people finally embrace, for she deemed it wise to beat a silent retreat and be safely back in her room with the light out before Alice returned to the house.

She managed to get to sleep at last, her mind calmed by the prospect of turning Sir Roderick against John, a task that was well within her powers. At half past six she rose as usual and hastened to perform her household tasks, in particular the preparation of a variety of dishes to lay on the sideboard for breakfast. Whatever her preoccupations, Letty was still a thorough and conscientious worker, and cooking was her art and joy. She placed the cat's morning saucer of milk on the kitchen floor without thinking, and then suddenly remembered and picked it up again.

"Oh. I'm not supposed to know," she muttered to herself, looking at the saucer. Except that I must know, she thought next, or I would not be able to tell Sir Roderick that the young man has gone off with the cat.

This was dreadfully complicated and puzzling. In fact the whole situation was fraught with pitfalls. She would have to keep her wits about her every moment and concentrate on the job she did so well: setting people against each other without their being able to prove she was doing it, and in particular fanning the flames of Sir Roderick's fury against John.

She put the saucer of milk back on the floor. Best to go on as usual for the moment and see how the land lay when the others appeared. The nurse was the first to do so. She was a tall, handsome woman of about Letty's age and with a very dictatorial manner. Her instructions from Alice were to prepare some weak tea and dry toast for the patient with her own hands, and she took over the kitchen for the purpose, treating Letty like a skivvy. By the time she had gone Letty felt her heart thumping and her head throbbing with rage.

"The snooty bitch," she muttered to herself. "I'll deal with the likes of her. I'll show her who's who and rub her nose in the dirt when I'm the ladyship myself."

She could actually see herself, in full splendour, contemptuously dismissing the now cringing nurse. This entrancing vision was interrupted by the smell of burning, and Letty rescued the grilled bacon only just in time. This was bad. She must keep her mind on the business in hand. She was playing for very high stakes and she would have to be very careful not to show her cards until the right moment had come.

Unfortunately for Letty, she had neither the brains nor the strength of character to take full advantage of her tantalizingly promising position. Her triumph over John the day before had made her overconfident; all genuine humility had deserted her, and she was quite incapable of making any realistic assessment of her chances of success. She was quite sure that she could so arrange things that John and Alice, and indeed the entire household, would find themselves at the receiving end of Sir Roderick's wrath, with only Letty herself good and loyal and true. At that point she might venture a tiny hint that it would be well for Sir Roderick if he kept in Letty's good books, because she knew what she knew.

It was a beautiful day-dream, far removed from any possible reality; but in the excitement of her discoveries and in her new-found sense of power, Letty did not distinguish between the two.

Next on the scene was Alice, looking pale and unhappy.

"Had a bad night, dear?" asked Letty sympathetically, following out Sir Roderick's policy of keeping the victim unsuspicious until the right moment came for the snap.

"I didn't sleep very well," was the reply. "I was worried about Auntie."

You're a bad liar, my girl, thought Letty as she put the finishing touches to the breakfast table; it's not your old auntie you're worried about, it's your young man. I'll spring it on them at breakfast, she decided, so that she doesn't have time to think up a convincing story before her uncle starts questioning her. Letty could contemplate the sacrifice of Alice without a qualm. Not that she had anything against the girl personally; Alice was friendly enough for someone of her class and carried her aristocratic haughtiness very lightly. Nor had Letty any really serious grudge against John, who was a fine-looking young fellow in spite of his low-class origins. In fact in different circumstances she might even have considered furthering their intrigue, relishing the delights of standing up for young love against the world, and earning the undying gratitude of them both. But as things now stood she had got to look after herself, and Alice must fight her own battles.

When Sir Roderick appeared Letty could see at once that he too had slept badly and was not in the sunniest of moods. Wisely she kept silent while she poured out his coffee. They all three ate cornflakes without speaking a word. But when Alice, after glancing at the hot dishes, said she didn't want any of them but would just have a piece of toast, her uncle scowled at her and said abruptly: "What's the matter with you?"

"Nothing," she replied equally curtly. "I don't have to eat if I don't want to."

Letty glanced from one to the other of them and then hid her glee by bending low over her eggs and bacon. She for one was going to make a good meal; she needed to keep up her strength.

"That damned interfering woman," said Sir Roderick presently. "Tried to keep me out of the bedroom early this morning when I looked in to see how she was. Not to be disturbed on any account, she said. As if I couldn't be trusted to have a quiet look at my own wife!"

"What time was this?" asked Alice.

"I don't know, Two, three, half past perhaps." Sir Roderick shrugged, pursed up his lips, and gave a display of a spoilt, sulky old man. "Who told her to act the little Hitler? That old ass Lethbridge?"

Alice simply shrugged in her turn and made no reply.

"She's a dreadfully bossy woman," ventured Letty. "Even more so than most nurses."

"She certainly is," said Sir Roderick, beaming upon the companion-help in order to aggravate his niece, and thereby giving Letty a great uplift of the heart and sending her day-dreams spinning afresh. "I hope we don't have to have her around the place for too long," he went on. "Of course it would mean additional work for you, my dear Letty, but as soon as Lady Heron is a little recovered—"

"I don't think we ought to send the nurse away just yet," broke in Alice, suddenly coming out of her trance and speaking with unwonted firmness. "The doctor said Auntie needed constant attention."

"No doubt," retorted her uncle. "One would, however, have supposed that two women in the house could have provided that without sending for a nurse. However, I was not consulted. As usual."

"Oh, Uncle Rod, that isn't fair!" cried Alice. "You know I'd love to look after Auntie and Letty never minds how much work she takes on, but Auntie didn't want either of us and you said yourself that you didn't want me sitting up all night."

"Maybe, maybe," said Sir Roderick vaguely, and then he smiled on Letty again. "A particularly nice scrambled egg. Did you do anything special with it?"

"No, not really," she replied. And then she had a little inspiration. "Are you quite sure," she asked Alice sweetly, "that you won't try a little scrambled egg? It slips down so easily. I don't think it could possibly hurt you."

Alice's refusal was really quite rude, which gave Letty a further opportunity.

"It's no good mourning over Quizzy, dear," she said. "He had to die some day, you know."

The effect of this remark exceeded her wildest hopes. Alice turned pale as death and Sir Roderick banged down his knife and fork on his plate and exclaimed: "What? What did you say? What's this about the cat?"

Letty put a hand to her mouth and glanced nervously from one to the other of them. "Oh dear," she murmured. "I'm ever so sorry, Sir Roderick. I thought you knew."

"It appears," he said very coldly, "that I am not only forbidden to see my wife but I am also to be kept in ignorance about the death of the family pet. Perhaps you will be kind enough—" he turned to Alice—"to inform me what has taken place. I believe I had your promise to see Quizzy safely in last night."

"I found him dead," muttered Alice, staring at the table. "Under the laburnum tree."

"Really? And where is he now?"

"I buried him." Alice's head dropped lower than ever. Her voice could scarcely be heard, but Letty's gasp of amazement was very audible indeed. Sir Roderick appeared equally astonished.

"And where," he asked, "did this most extraordinary midnight interment take place? And what implement did you use? And did you not find it an intolerable strain on the nerves, to dig a grave for your aunt's pet and place the corpse in it and cover it up with earth, all by yourself, unaided, and in the darkness of the night?"

"I managed," mumbled Alice. "I thought it the best thing to do, to save Auntie being too upset."

At this Sir Roderick had simply raised his eyebrows and helped himself to toast and marmalade. The meal concluded in silence, but when Letty rose to clear away and Alice started to help her, Sir Roderick remarked with the same icy sarcasm as before: "I believe Letty is capable of managing without your assistance. If you could spare a moment from these peculiar tasks that you appear to be setting yourself nowadays, perhaps you would kindly come along to the den and type that letter I mentioned last night."

"All right," said Alice, very sulkily in Letty's opinion.

Letty cleared everything out of the dining-room as quickly as she could and then went to listen at the keyhole of Sir Roderick's room. It took some courage, but she had an excuse ready, and she felt tolerably safe now that the full blast of his fury was directed towards his niece. Letty could not remember having seen Sir Roderick quite so furious with Alice before, not even when the battle about her leaving home to go and live in her friend's flat had been at its height.

There was a tremendous battle going on now, behind the closed door of Sir Roderick's room. Letty's eyes opened wider as she listened.

"But why on earth couldn't you tell me straight," she heard Alice cry, "that you wouldn't leave me any money unless I marry Cousin Lionel? It's really too mean of you, Uncle, honestly it is, to say nothing until I type the letter to the solicitor altering your will!"

Sir Roderick's response was much what Letty would have expected. "Do you seriously think," she heard him say, "that a girl brought up as you have been, having everything you have ever asked for, is going to settle down happily on a schoolmaster's wages?"

Alice said something here that Letty could not catch.

"Oh yes," went on her uncle raising his voice. "I know all about the grand gesture of independence and the playing at housekeeping in Meg's little flat which is such a convenient place to meet your young man. I've nothing against him personally, mind, and even you can hardly accuse me of not being friendly and making him welcome. But you are not going to marry him and that's flat. And in fairness to the boy himself I think you ought to tell him the contents of this letter."

"It won't make any difference!" cried Alice. "He doesn't care about my money."

"Oh, come off it," said Sir Roderick brutally. "Don't give me that stuff. You know nothing whatever about men—particularly young ones with ambition—and I'll grant the youngster that. He's got some stuffing in him. Might even make some sort of a name for himself one day. But he is not for you and Lionel is. You've always liked him and you know it has always been my dearest wish." The voice had softened and Letty could well imagine that Sir Roderick was now appearing as a pathetic old man. "You know what it has meant to me to have no son or daughter, and you know that I care more for you than for anyone in the world. If I could see you and Lionel married then I should die happy. That's all I have left to hope for."

Letty did not hear Alice's response to this particular piece of emotional blackmail, because at that moment the sound of a door opening on the floor above sent her flying back to the kitchen to get on with her work before the nurse came out of Lady Heron's room. She thought hard as she tidied up the kitchen, going over all the possibilities inherent in the conversation that she had just overheard. If only that silly young fool John would co-operate they could blackmail Sir Roderick beautifully, the two of them. And with much greater safety than Letty could achieve on her own. For by this time a little cold dash of reality was beginning to disturb her dream. It started when she heard Sir Roderick shouting at his niece, whom there was no doubt he dearly loved, but even that didn't save her. Letty would not have liked at all to be in Alice's shoes at that moment. Could it perhaps be that the price of a title and splendour and luxury for the rest of her days was too high a one to pay if it meant standing up to the full force of Sir Roderick's rage with nobody to help her and nobody else present on whom to divert it?

As she swept through her morning work, Letty's dreams began to take on a rather different character, one a little more in accordance with reality. If the highest peak was too dangerous to climb, how about contenting herself with the money instead. She had got to do something. The knowledge that she had in her possession was too precious to waste. She would drop a little hint as soon as she could. At the very least she would get a rise in her none too generous salary, and at best she would get hold of a substantial sum of money, enough to buy a little hat shop perhaps, and set up in business on her own. She had always prided herself on having a good eye for a smart hat.

And when she was independent she could cook what she liked and when she liked, she thought as she prepared the lunch. It was always fish on Fridays at Blenheim Close, not because any of the family had strong religious principles, but because it always had been that way. When she had her own little shop she could make herself a nice steak-and-kidney pie for Friday's dinner if she felt like it. What a luxury that would be.

At about a quarter to one Sir Roderick came in as usual to enquire what was on the menu. He had been shut up in his room ever since the row with his niece, and Alice herself had fled to her own bedroom at the top of the house and had not emerged since. Letty imagined her sobbing her heart out on the bed.

"Halibut," said Sir Roderick, nodding approval. He was quite amicable again and seemed to want to be friendly. "The cat would have liked that," he added.

"Yes indeed," said Letty, trying to compose her features

into an expression of mourning and hoping that she sounded suitably distressed.

"I am wondering what is the best thing to do," he went on, "about breaking the news to Lady Heron. She appears to be a lot better this morning—I have at last been permitted by that dragon to have a look at her—but of course this will be a very grave shock to her. What is your opinion, Letty?"

"I really couldn't say," said Letty primly.

"Apparently she has asked for Quizzy," said Sir Roderick, "but the nurse has taken it upon herself to forbid the animal in the sickroom. Really she is the most high-handed woman I have ever had the misfortune to encounter. A little bit of decent humility and respect even in a nurse would not come amiss. However. The problem is how to break the bad news to Lady Heron, and to deal with the request that she will no doubt make, to have a sight of the corpse, since that will now scarcely be practicable in view of Alice's extraordinary behaviour. Burying the cat! What a thing to do! And without telling anybody."

"Well, as a matter of fact," said Letty slowly, and then she took the plunge. The temptation was too great. Such an opportunity might not occur again. Had she been as alert as she usually was to the nuances of her employer's behaviour, had she listened more to his tone of voice and less to the actual words that he spoke, she might have guessed that in fact Sir Roderick was not nearly as displeased as he had seemed to be about Alice's action; in fact Letty might even have detected a faint note of complacency. But her mind had been working so hard at its own plans that her antennae were less sensitive than usual. She believed that he was furious with Alice both on account of the cat and on account of her fondness for John, and that it would most certainly profit her, Letty, to keep his anger on the boil against both the young people.

"I really do feel that perhaps you ought to know," she said, "that dear Alice was not—well, not quite correct in what she said about the cat."

"Not correct? What d'you mean?"

Letty took a deep breath and spoke quickly before her courage ran out.

"I heard a noise outside my bedroom window last night and I looked out and saw someone going along carrying something large and I thought I had better see what it was so I came down and heard the two of them, Alice and the young man, by the front gate talking about him taking away the cat's body to find out what killed him."

Sir Roderick's reaction to this statement was something that Letty hoped she would one day be able to forget. Never in her life had she seen anybody in such a towering rage and the names he called her made her blood run cold. Desperately clutching at any straw with which to defend herself, she hinted that he had better be careful what he said to her because she knew something about his past that he would much rather she didn't know.

At that all hell had broken loose and she had afterwards only the most confused recollection of what had in fact taken place. Alice and the nurse had both rushed downstairs and Jimmy had rushed in from the garden, and between the three of them they had dragged the old man away from her and held him for a moment or two, and in that moment or two of reprieve she had snatched up the black bag that still contained the precious letters, grabbed her hat and coat that were in the hall and struggled to put them on as she ran in the pouring rain along towards the pedestrian way that led from the far end of Blenheim Close into the University Parks. Once there, she paused in the shelter of a tree to draw breath and to take stock of the situation.

She had escaped from the house with her life and with the

letters and that was a lot to be thankful for, but there was no use thinking it was safe to rest for long. She would not go back to that house, no, never, not if a fortune lay there for the picking up. There was a woman she knew slightly who kept a boarding-house up Cowley way; that might be a temporary refuge. And she had quite a tidy sum in the Post Office Savings Bank, so she could take her time about finding another job. Perhaps it would be a good idea to try a school or a college this time. A men students' hostel, for instance, with a kindly grey-haired bachelor as warden . . .

Letty came out from under the shelter of the tree, her mind momentarily chasing a new dream. The relentless rain brought her back to the reality of her present position. It was not safe to linger too long in the neighbourhood of Blenheim Close; she certainly didn't fancy walking back past the house to wait for a bus in the main road. She had better go along the river walk, although it was a long way and the weather was terrible. At any rate it would give her time to collect her wits and try to decide what to do about those letters.

It would be a dreadful shame to waste them completely, after all the trouble they had cost her. If only she could think of a safe place to put them for the time being, for she really could not carry them about with her everywhere, never daring to let go of her bag if anybody else was about. What did people do when they had a treasure and wanted to be able to get hold of it again without anyone else knowing that they had got it? Sew it up inside a mattress? Bury it in the ground?

Letty plodded wearily along the now deserted banks of the River Cherwell, her clothes becoming wetter and wetter every moment, her mind a ragbag of ideas: such a charming elderly don—"how good you are with the students, Miss

Mann"; a nice cup of tea and get out of these wet clothes; the little hat shop after all if she played her cards right; and everything she had ever read or heard about secret hiding-places for treasure.

10

"Thanks a lot, Graham," said John over the phone. "It's just what I suspected."

And now I have to face Alice, he thought, without any time to decide what line to take with her and whether or not to go on pretending.

"I've patched up the poor old boy as well as I could," Graham was saying, "in case your friends want to give him a funeral as we used to do as kids when the dog died. A little weep and a couple of sticks with a bit of cardboard saying 'Here lies Rover—dear old pal.' Silly rather, but it softened the blow."

"That was a good idea," said John, touched by this truly thoughtful piece of kindness on the part of the stolid scientist, but not quite knowing how, in terms of their casual friendship, to express his own gratitude. "You're quite a dear old pal yourself. I do appreciate it."

He became conscious then of a slight movement behind him, and finished the conversation in a hurry.

"Got to go now. There's a fresh crisis arisen. See you this evening. Thanks again."

He turned round to face Alice, who had come quietly up the basement stairs.

"You don't need to tell me," she said, with a face bleak as a barren rock. "I know all about it. I guessed it from the first."

"But why, why?" asked John, holding his hands stiffly to his sides. They were aching to reach out to her, but the barriers were up again between them and the moment when she had rushed into his arms crying for his help might just as well have never been.

She shrugged. "Experimenting perhaps. Or sheer bloody-mindedness."

John stared at her. There was a lightness in her tone that deceived him for a moment. And then he saw beneath the surface. To face bitter disillusionment about someone you dearly loved was not much fun, as who should know better than himself? He even managed to refrain from comment when she went on, talking to herself as much as to him: "When you've been used to wielding authority on a large scale, it must be very difficult to come down to a small sphere of operations, and if you so much enjoy exercising power over other people you tend to try to find other ways . . ."

Her voice tailed away. In a moment, thought John, she was going to plead that her uncle was not quite sane, which of course in a way he wasn't, although it would be totally impossible to prove it. But in fact she came out with a remark which greatly startled him and threw the ball right back into his court.

"Why did you tell me last night that you believed he had killed Emily Witherington?" she demanded.

"How on earth . . ." he began, and then it dawned on him. That bit of paper on which he had been working out the case against Sir Roderick; he had left it lying on his desk for anyone to see. The most casual of glances would have taken in its contents; it was not necessary for her to do any deliberate spying. She had probably noticed the tumbled typescript of his book scattered over the desk and had gone to put it together. It would not be the first time she had brought some order into his untidy habits of working.

"I'm sorry," he said, looking away. "It was very careless of me to leave those notes lying about."

"Careless!" she cried furiously. "Is that all you can say? You've got this thing boiling away in your mind and you don't breathe a word of it to me and all you can do is apologize for being careless! What the hell do you think I am? A babe in arms? A schoolgirl? One of your Victorian young ladies who is too innocent to be told about the wickedness of men? What sort of person do you take me for, what sort of standards and values do you think I've got? Do you really believe that I would put family loyalty and affection above the claims of justice and truth?"

John was speechless. Alice lowered her voice a little and went on: "I'm disappointed in you, John. I thought we were on equal terms and could face things together. I've been doing—" and her voice trembled for a moment—"I've been doing quite a bit of facing things on my own. But what's the point of it if all you do is treat me like a child too?"

John muttered some sort of apology. Of all the shocks that he had piling up on him over the last days, the shock of Alice rounding on him in this way was the very worst. He had never loved or admired her more and yet he dared not touch her; he did not know how to defend himself or how to try to explain himself.

"We'd better be going," he said, opening the front door.

They looked out together into the streaming rain.

"I'll ring for a taxi," he said.

"Yes," she agreed absent-mindedly, and then went on: "I do wish we had the use of a car." She caught sight of Mrs. Willey's old Morris standing at the kerb. "Let's take it, John. She's let you borrow it before."

"Not without asking," he said.

"She won't mind when she hears how important it is," said Alice impatiently. "Have you got a key?"

Without another word John opened the little drawer in the hall table and took out the spare ignition key. Then he scribbled a brief note for his landlady.

"I don't want to smash it up for her," he remarked as they drove away.

"There's no reason why we should," said Alice. "It's only so that we can get around quickly if necessary. If anything does happen to it I'll buy her another."

John made no reply. It was he who was boiling over with resentment now. Buy her another! Just like that, as if they were borrowing a pint of milk. An elderly widow's battered old car, that her husband had looked after carefully and on which she now spent a good part of her pension so that she could tootle about visiting her friends. Buy her another. Why, it would take John himself years to save up for an old banger like Mrs. Willey's, but for Alice it meant no more than her signature on a cheque.

Was this what a life with Alice would be like? All right, so she had played down her wealth and prospects up till now, he had to grant her that. They had gone equal shares in all their amusements and she had never once suggested doing anything that he could not afford, nor made him feel that she was depriving herself of some comfort in order to come down to his level. She had sat in cheap seats at the theatre and cinema, eaten at cheap restaurants, gone for bus rides with him. And all as if it was a completely natural thing for her to do, and without a trace of condescension, without the least air of royalty slumming it just for a lark. But she was showing up in her true colours now. The family crisis was bringing out all the innate arrogance of her. If she accused him of keeping his suspicions about her uncle to himself, could he not equally accuse her of putting on a false personality to deceive him?

He smothered his own discomfiture by whipping himself up into a fine state of fury at her duplicity, and they drove the short distance to Blenheim Close in an uncomfortable silence. As they drew up at Number Eleven John glanced sideways and saw that she was quietly crying. Resentment melted. She really was in great distress, and after all she could not help her birth and wealth. He put an arm round her and murmured reassurances as he had so often done before. But this time she was not to be comforted. She blinked and blew her nose and shook herself.

"I'm sorry," she said coolly. "That was very feeble of me. I will try not to do it again. I feel better now. Thank you for coming. It's very decent of you, considering what you have found out about my uncle." She drew away from him. "I am very sorry indeed that you should have been dragged into my unhappy family affairs. It should not last much longer, however, and then you'll be rid of us."

"But Alice, but darling . . ." John started to protest and found he was talking to air. She had slipped out the passenger side and was already opening the gate. He thought she would look back and smile at him or at any rate beckon him in, but she simply walked on towards the house. A memory from boyhood struck at him with a sharp new pain and he was conscious of an intolerable sense of loss. Surely this could not be the end of it all between them? It had all happened so suddenly. At one moment they had

seemed to be completely reconciled and he had been full of
grand quixotic notions of trying to spare Alice the knowledge of her uncle's crime, and now here they were
apparently going to part for ever as soon as this immediate
crisis had been resolved.

Where had he gone wrong? Surely it could not be all his
own fault? If he had told Alice last night about his
suspicions, her reactions would have been very different
from what they were now. Look at the way she had behaved
at first over the cat. Something must have happened to make
her alter her views; something connected with the row that
had blown up and sent her rushing to him for help. She
really had been frightened, though she was hiding it now,
and if it had not been for their stupid quarrel he would have
learnt by now what it was all about.

"Uncle's gone berserk," she had said, and as far as he
had been able to take in her words at all at that moment, he
had taken this for a figure of speech, meaning that Sir
Roderick had been laying into the lot of them with the lash
of his tongue. Could it be even worse? Had the old man
really gone right round the bend and threatened physical
violence? With Alice herself in danger? Why, if anyone
ever tried to lay a hand on Alice . . .

John followed her into the house with his muscles tensed
and his mind full of the craziest longings to perform heroic
deeds on her behalf. But there was no maniac rapist or
murderer lurking in the hall on whom he could display his
courage and prove his love for Alice. There was not even a
furious great-uncle on the rampage. There was only a tall,
soberly-dressed woman speaking on the telephone in a most
indignant voice.

"Really, Doctor, I have never been so insulted in all my
life, and in a titled household too! I am not accustomed to
such treatment. A certain amount of impatience and short-

ness of temper is quite natural where there is anxiety over illness. I trust I am not uncharitable or intolerant, and I hope I know enough of human nature to realize that allowances have to be made, but if you had heard the way he carried on!"

There was a short pause, and then she resumed: "Very well, then. I will stay here for another hour, but not one minute after that. If you have not succeeded in obtaining a replacement by then I am going to leave this house, patient or no patient, duty or no duty. I will not stay here to be insulted like that again, and if you'll take my advice you'll send a bodyguard along with the next nurse—preferably an ex-heavyweight boxer."

She slammed down the receiver and turned to confront Alice and John, who had involuntarily crept closer to each other as they listened to her talking.

"Oh. So you're back, Miss Heron," said the nurse. "You heard what I said to Dr. Lethbridge?"

"Yes," replied Alice coldly. "I am sorry you have been subjected to such a disagreeable experience. There is no need for you to remain here another hour. I will look after my aunt myself."

"Oh no, I wouldn't want you to do that," said the nurse, changing her tune. "I'm sure the doctor will send somebody else along soon. I had to lay it on a bit thick with him, you see, because he's inclined to be rather dilatory, but of course I didn't really mean that I would desert Lady Heron."

"It doesn't matter in the slightest what you meant or didn't mean," said Alice even more icily than before. "We have no further need of your services and I shall be grateful if you will kindly leave the house."

"Well, really." The nurse drew a deep breath in preparation for another offended speech and John, who had withdrawn just inside the dining-room door, listened to the ensuing battle with interest and with spirits suddenly remarkably revived. He felt like cheering Alice on to victory. She was indeed turning out to be a true Heron, arrogant and formidable and unbending, but he couldn't help admiring her all the same. After a few more skirmishes the nurse had to acknowledge defeat, and she went upstairs with Alice to collect her things with a very bad grace. When the front door had closed behind her John emerged from his retreat, longing to applaud but feeling it would be more tactful not to.

"Now, what did your uncle actually do?" he asked.

Alice gave a brief and severely edited account of the events of the morning.

"Letty must have heard us or seen us last night," she said, "and chosen the worst moment to tell Uncle you'd taken the cat away. She was brewing up for it at breakfast and I ought to have tried to prevent it, but I had other problems."

John did not ask what these problems had been; he believed he could guess. Perhaps one day they would talk openly to each other about it after all, but meanwhile there was a job to be done for which he must keep cool and try not to lose his temper.

"Did Letty take her black handbag with her?" he asked.

"I didn't notice. I'll go and look."

Alice ran upstairs while John searched the kitchen and the drawing-room. They met again in the hall, shaking their heads at each other.

"If she's taken it with her," began John and then stopped.

Her eyes were challenging him; he could still hear the ring of her passionate plea not to be treated like a child.

"Then I think Letty's life may be in danger," he concluded.

— 11 —

"Yes," said Alice in an expressionless voice.

"Where would she go?" said John, frowning and biting his lip. He was dying to be doing something, but there was little point in rushing off to drive about the streets of Oxford without having the least notion in which direction Letty had gone.

A loud tapping sound came from the floor above.

"Auntie's stick," said Alice. "I must see what she wants."

"I'll come too," said John. It had occurred to him that Lady Heron, who knew so much, might be able to help with this problem too. Provided she had the strength to talk, of course, after all the excitements of the day.

He held Alice back at the foot of the stairs. "Does she know about Quizzy?" he whispered.

Alice shook her head. "Don't let on. Pretend you saw him in the garden if she asks. I'll tell her after you've gone."

He squeezed her hand. "Good girl. Keep going. We'll beat this thing."

She gave him the briefest of smiles but he knew that he had been forgiven.

Lady Heron was propped up against the pillows. The only life left in her seemed to be that in her eyes. But her voice, too, was surprisingly firm. "Hurry up, you two," she said as they came into the room. "Sit down, John. I'd like a little clear soup, Alice. Could you make me some straight away?"

Alice moved towards the door.

"And thank you for getting rid of that harpy for me," cried her aunt. "Now, John," she went on when Alice had left the room. "This is a mess, isn't it? Do I take it that Letty has managed to get hold of those letters?"

John explained briefly what had happened.

"The poor fool," said Lady Heron. "They'll be the death of her."

She seemed to wilt for a moment, and John could see how frail she really was and guessed that it was willpower alone that was keeping her going.

Lady Heron roused herself. "We've got to stop this somehow. She's a vicious little sneak thief but she still doesn't deserve to be murdered. Besides, I don't want my husband hanged during my lifetime."

No, but you wouldn't mind it after your death, mentally added John, and he could not help thinking that that event could not be very far distant.

"Does he know these letters still exist?" he asked.

"He didn't up till now. They've been sealed up at the bank for years, in a box with some jewellery. The clerk who brought them out to me thought it was only the jewels. I arranged it for one afternoon when my husband was taking the chair at a local charity meeting. But Letty must have twigged something, and I wasn't as careful as I should have been. He'll have guessed it all by now. She lost no time trying to blackmail him, the imbecile. Talk about fools rushing in . . . Never mind. Let's think what she'll do now."

"Put the letters in a bank perhaps."

"It's too late. They're all shut by now."

"A solicitor's office?"

"She wouldn't trust them. And neither would I. Some inquisitive clerk would read the lot."

"How about somebody more trustworthy, then. A parson? Does she go to church?" asked John.

"Yes. St. Andrew's. Very High Church. There's great drama Sunday mornings if she misses early service. It's just possible that she's feeling scared enough to want to confess."

John made as if to stand up. "Then I'd better go and see the vicar."

"No. Wait a moment. Let's think this out thoroughly."

John waited.

"It depends how frightened she is, and whether she fully realizes her danger," said Lady Heron.

"If she was all that frightened she could always go to the police."

"And tell them what? That she was trying to blackmail her employer and he lost his temper with her?"

John had to admit that this was a difficulty.

"No. I think she will hang on to the letters so that she can try again," went on Lady Heron. "I know that woman. She's like a limpet once she gets a notion into her head. And her head's stuffed with all sorts of romantic nonsense."

"Has she any close friends?" asked John, after the old woman had remained silent for a few moments.

She regarded him with an ironic look faintly reminiscent of her husband. "Do you think it likely?"

"No, I suppose not." If John had not been relieved of the letters, he decided, he would have given them to Graham for temporary safe-keeping, knowing he could trust him, and would finally have handed them over to Professor Woodward. But then he was lucky to have good friends and advisers, and it was rather shocking to think there were people who were totally without them.

"When I gave them to you," said Lady Heron, "I knew I could trust you not to make use of them purely for your own purposes. But Letty has the nature and instincts of a blackmailer. I'm quite sure she'll put them somewhere safe and try again later from a distance. The point is, where."

"She's got to spend the night somewhere," said John. "She'll have to rent a room or go to a hotel."

"Possibly."

They both thought in silence for a moment.

"Go into her room," commanded Lady Heron, "and look for a clue. See what she's been reading. She might lift an idea from one of her love stories."

John did as she bade him and returned with a small volume whose appearance was very familiar to him indeed. It had a public library label inside the front cover and there was a slip of paper inserted at a page about half-way through. "It was on her bedside table," he said.

"Emily Witherington's last book of poems," said Lady Heron, taking it out of his hands. "So she'd searched for evidence there. She's brighter than I took her for, is our Letty."

They opened the book together at the marked page and together they read the poem silently.

"'Bird in Flight,'" said John at last. "The ride down from the top of Boar's Hill. It's clear enough why Letty marked that one. But does it help us now? Would she actually go there? Surely there's nowhere up Boar's Hill where she could safely hide a bundle of letters? Unless she digs a hole under a hedge and buries them."

"It sounds unlikely," said Lady Heron, "but she's a romantic idiot. It's not impossible. And Roderick obviously thinks she's gone some distance or he wouldn't have taken the car."

"But Letty would have to go by bus."

"Or taxi. Or pinch somebody's bike. She's pretty desperate. It's a very long shot, but I can't think of anything better."

Lady Heron, whose voice had been becoming more and more faint during this last speech, suddenly fell back against the pillow, utterly exhausted. John murmured that he would do his best and then left the room. At the bottom of the stairs he met Alice, who looked at him enquiringly.

"She thinks Letty may have gone up Boar's Hill," said John, "following a clue from the poems, and she wants me to drive up there and look for her."

"Sounds very doubtful to me," said Alice.

"To me too, but we've got to do something, and I can't think of anything else."

He moved to the front door and Alice came forward and caught his hand. "Take care of yourself," she said softly. "Drive carefully."

"And you take care of yourself too." He gripped her shoulders for a moment and then released her. "Equal partners," he said, giving her a wide grin and a thumbs-up signal as he went through the door.

He turned Mrs. Willey's car round in the road and drove off in a southerly direction. In the heavy traffic of Cornmarket he sat fretting with impatience, and at the same time feeling less and less confident about the direction of his search. He had found it very difficult to think clearly under Lady Heron's eager scrutiny, but away from it his own judgement reasserted itself. It was senseless to go on; there was nothing but a constantly-changing landscape of road-works at the place where Emily died. It would be as sensible to try to hide something there as to bury your treasure in a volcano. Lady Heron hardly ever went out now; she would not realize how everything had changed.

John turned out of the traffic as soon as he could and found a spot where he could park for a minute or two and lit a cigarette. Supposing it had been he himself, and not Letty, who had rushed from the house in a panic but determined to keep the treasure. What could he have done, assuming he had nowhere to go to, no trusted friend to whom to turn, and a deep-rooted suspicion of lawyers and all officialdom? And supposing he was a romantically-minded person and had just been reading Emily's poems and pondering deeply upon them and upon the love of her life? What struck one most about her poems? The bird imagery, for one thing. Even a reader like Letty, totally unversed in the techniques of literary criticism, could not fail to notice how much there was about the sensation of flying and about the haven of the nest. But that idea had led nowhere.

What else? The garden. No good. There would be no hiding of anything in the garden at Blenheim Close. The river walk? The hollow tree? But of course. Why on earth had he and Lady Heron not thought of it when they were reading the poems. The lovers in the poem leaving messages for each other in one of nature's own hiding-places; why, there was even a hint of it in one of the letters themselves. Surely Letty would have liked that bit and would have remembered it.

John threw away his cigarette and started up the engine. It was another long shot of course, but a more plausible one than Boar's Hill. At least Letty could go on her own two feet to that part of the riverbank where the old willows grew; she would not need to take taxis or nick bicycles or go for long country walks in the rain.

He left the car at the southernmost entrance to the University Parks and set out systematically to inspect every old tree in the neighbourhood. It was a formidable task, in this region of willows, and for a moment he though of enlisting Graham's help, but dropped the idea because it would waste precious time. Luckily the rain had died down to a drizzle by now, and he trudged grimly along in the damp grass by the side of the river in the deserted Parks, inspecting one tree after another.

Having exhausted that stretch of the bank, he made his way across the bridge to the narrow pathway between the two waters, and groaned as he saw the daunting number of new possibilities ahead of him. Not only was he now thoroughly tired and wet, but he was also very hungry, having been surviving since breakfast on one cup of coffee and a biscuit and a very big diet of apprehension and anxiety. The vision of one of Letty's delicious savouries rose up to tantalize him, but almost immediately afterwards he thought: if she ever cooks anything again, and he struggled on with what was beginning to look more and more like a futile hunt.

And then at last, almost at the far end of the narrow river walk, near to the path that would bring him out to the eastern sector of the city, he found what he was seeking—a rotten pollard willow, right on the water's edge, with a few bright green shoots round the base showing that the sap still flowed within that dried-up hulk. There was a large hole in the bark and a deep cavity inside. John put his hand in and felt around rather gingerly, for he had a great dislike of spiders. There seemed to be nothing there that one would not expect to find in such a place.

He leant against the trunk, stared at the melancholy scene of grey skies and dripping trees and muddy waters and repeated Emily's poem to himself. She must have stood here like this, on just such a dismal afternoon in spring, and despaired almost to the point of flinging herself into the water. He could feel her feeling it, with every bit of his heart and mind. At one moment he almost believed that he saw her, a shadowy form in a long loose gown, coming towards him along the path.

He stood up straight again and shook himself and swore. This was no more Emily's tree than the daffodils blooming near Rydalwater on his Easter visit to the Lake District had been Wordsworth's daffodils. He was letting his imagination run away with him, as he used to be accused of doing when he was a child. Emily's old tree would have crumbled into the river and drifted away; this was just an old stump that answered the same description, and there was nothing in it, and he was sick to death of all these searches and mysteries, past and present alike, and nothing in the world mattered to him in the least except to get out of these wet clothes and sit down to a big plateful of steak and chips.

He walked on for a few yards before finally turning back and exclaiming aloud: "I'm giving up."

And then he saw it. Almost concealed by the young leafage of an overhanging hawthorn bush, and held back by the bush from the flow of the stream, floated a most incongruous object. It was a little straw hat with a narrow brim and a drooping feather, and it was dyed a peculiarly repulsive shade of pink.

John broke off a long stick from a tree, bent over the end, hooked it round the hat and pulled it towards him. Then he climbed back up the bank on to the path and stood thoughtfully holding it at arm's length. Surely he could not be mistaken in thinking that Letty was its owner. He knew very few women who wore hats at all, and he knew that he was not observant about clothes, but the moment when he had come away from Mrs. Willey's broken-down car to see Letty standing on the doorstep was still very fresh in his mind. He could remember himself thinking that Alice would never wear such a ghastly colour. He would not like to swear in court that this was Letty's hat, but in the circumstances it seemed a fair enough supposition, and he didn't think that in this case he was letting his imagination play tricks with him. The hat must have been a favourite of hers, he thought, to be remembered even at the moment when she had run in terror from the house.

Must have been. John realized that he had used the past tense in his mind. He had instantly jumped to the conclusion that Letty was dead. But her hat floating in the water was only evidence that she had been near this spot; it did not necessarily mean that she had drowned. And even if she was found drowned, it was not necessarily murder. She could have been scrambling about on the wet slippery bank looking for the hollow tree and been unable to save herself from falling into the river. If she couldn't swim and if there was no human being within call, as there surely wasn't, then it would be easy enough to drown. And there was yet another explanation that one could not completely rule out. Perhaps in her fright and despair she had been momentarily overcome by the urge to finish it all and had jumped into the river of her own volition.

John put all these arguments to himself as he stood looking with distaste at the hat, but all the same he could not help feeling quite sure both that Sir Roderick had contrived Letty's death and that there would not be the slightest shred of evidence against him. He poked about under the hawthorn branches for a few minutes longer and prodded at the wet grass on the bank, but he soon abandoned these activities, for really he had no idea what he was looking for. This was no longer a job for the amateur investigator; it was a job for the police. A woman had disappeared—there was no need to explain in exactly what circumstances—and it was up to the police to look for her. Alice would agree to that; she would tell him herself that this was the right course to take now.

He ran back along the river walk to where he had left the car, making good progress in spite of the dampness of the ground, and gripping Letty's pink hat in his right hand. Then he drove straight to the police station, handed over the hat, and tried to explain that he had found it in the river, where he believed Miss Mann had been walking in a state of great distress after being given notice from her job. After a seemingly endless series of irrelevant questions and other delays he managed to get the gist of his story out at last, only to realize that they were treating the whole thing as a bit of a student rag and not taking him seriously at all.

"But I'm not an undergraduate," he cried at last in despair to the stolid elderly sergeant who was interviewing him. "I'm a Research Fellow. Surely Oxford police ought to know the difference! Look, if you want to check up on my bona fides ring up my Professor, or better still, ring Lady Heron herself or her niece. They're personal friends of mine. It's on their account that I've got caught up in this business in the first place. They were awfully worried about Miss Mann and Lady Heron herself suggested that I should go out and look for her and made various suggestions about where she might have gone."

"And what about Sir Roderick Heron?" asked the sergeant. "What were his instructions?"

It was only too plain that he still suspected that the whole thing was some sort of elaborate hoax. John felt the sickening cold clutch of despair. Sir Roderick Heron, even in old age, was well-known in every section of the community. He was a big name. He had wealth and respect and authority and his word was beyond suspicion. Whatever chance had an obscure research student, even one with a blameless record and with the backing of his academic superior, against such a force as that? His story against Sir Roderick's—why, he hadn't a hope. What sort of naïve fool had he been to come straight to the police and believe that they would take some action instead of going back to Blenheim Close and confronting Sir Roderick himself with the hat and with his story?

But perhaps the old man had not yet returned. Perhaps he was still driving around somewhere establishing his own alibi. If only the sergeant would agree to talk to Lady Heron or to Alice on the phone there might be hope yet. They would back him up; they must do, they must. They couldn't enlist his help and then leave him floundering like this.

"As far as I know Sir Roderick and his chauffeur are still driving about looking for Miss Mann," said John as calmly as he could. "But if he's back by now I'm sure he would like to know at once about my finding this hat. Why don't you give him a ring?"

This produced some sort of impression at last, and he waited in tense impatience while the call was put through.

"Is that Miss Heron?" the sergeant said, and John's hopes rose. "I am very sorry to trouble you, ma'am, but we have here at the police station a young man of the name of John Broome who informs us that Sir Roderick Heron sent him out to look for your housekeeper, who there was some reason to suppose might have come to some harm. Is that correct?"

John gritted his teeth and clenched his hands into fists. Oh, Alice, Alice, he prayed, put them on to your aunt!

"I see," said the sergeant a moment later. "You have news of the missing lady so you don't wish us to take any action but you wish Mr. Broome to come and see you at once. Is that correct?"

John's hands relaxed. At least Sir Roderick wasn't back and Alice had turned up trumps and soothed down the police and given them all a second chance. But the next moment he felt his stomach contract with alarm again, because the tone of the sergeant's voice had changed; it had become even more deferential than before, and he was saying: "Yes sir, yes, Sir Roderick . . . No, I quite understand that your niece did not fully appreciate . . . yes indeed, sir. We will certainly hold Mr. Broome here until you come. Certainly, sir. I quite understand that in the circumstances you would prefer to come round and collect him and explain to him yourself. I am glad to hear that your housekeeper is visiting friends and is perfectly well, but sorry that you have been subjected to the annoyance of a student prank . . . ah well, sir, as you say, boys will be boys, and we were once young ourselves . . . very good of you to take it that way, sir, if I may say so . . . then you do not wish us to charge him . . . very generous of you, sir . . . yes indeed, he will be here ready for you to pick up in ten minutes. No, we won't let him go."

The sergeant replaced the receiver and turned to John with a tolerant smile and a cautionary wagging of the forefinger.

"You're lucky to get out of it so easily this time, young man," he said. "Very decent old gentleman, Sir Roderick Heron is. Very tolerant and understanding of young blood. But that's a new one on me, that is. That's a funny bit of a lark. Going off with the housekeeper's hat and pretending you'd found it where she'd gone and drowned herself in the river!" He shook his head. "That's quite a new one. Shows a bit of imagination, that does. Not like dressing up as a foreign potentate or shinning up the Martyrs' Memorial to place a certain domestic utensil on the top of it as they used to do in my young days. The housekeeper's hat!" He gave that object a contemptuous push. "That's a good one, that is."

John heard him in silence. Should he try and make a dash for it, he wondered. No, because they would only drag him back and he would then have put himself in the wrong with the law. Then I simply have to sit here, he decided, and wait to be picked up by a murderer and be placed at his mercy with the full consent and approval of the law, and then I wait to see in which way he intends to dispose of me.

But Alice knows, he thought, struggling with the waves of horror and of incredulity that hit at him alternately: Alice knows everything now; surely she will try to rescue me.

——·*12*·——

Sir Roderick's reception at the police station would have nauseated John had he not been so sickened already that nothing could make it worse. The old man's sunny geniality only highlighted John's own silent sullenness, no doubt confirming the police in their belief that he was sulking at being caught out in a silly rag. Viewed dispassionately, it was a splendid performance on the part of the old man, totally convincing to all except those very few people who were really in the know.

Miss Mann, Sir Roderick explained, had left the house rather abruptly after a misunderstanding. His wife and niece had been rather worried about her—these women, you know, and their young friend here who had come to consult Sir Roderick about a matter connected with his future career, had volunteered to go out and seek the missing lady. Meanwhile Miss Mann herself had telephoned from a friend's house to say she would be back in time to cook dinner, and he, Sir Roderick Heron, had actually asked his chauffeur to get out the car and drive around a little in the hope of finding the young man and saving him the trouble of continuing with an unnecessary search.

As for the hat, Sir Roderick looked at it with some distaste, remarked that he believed Miss Mann had one not unlike it, and gave an eloquent shrug of the shoulders as if to say that he himself would never have thought it necessary to come along to the police station with a cock-and-bull story about a woman being drowned if all the evidence he could produce was a hat that might or might not belong to the woman in question and that might have got into the water in any one of a dozen perfectly innocent ways.

Anyone listening to him who had not known John Broome well, would certainly have gained the impression that the young man had been driven by some grudge or other, by envy or unrequited love or some other disappointment, or even by Socialist idealism, to play a foolish trick upon the Herons, hoping, perhaps, to bring them a little disagreeable publicity; and they would have been equally impressed by the kindly tolerance of the old man towards the perpetrator of this bit of nonsense.

By the time they left the police station John was almost beginning to doubt his own reason and the evidence of his own senses. In the end it was quite a relief to step into the back of the Daimler and sink down on to the springy seat. At least between himself and Sir Roderick who sat by his side, and Jimmy in front, there need be no more of this disgusting charade.

As they turned into St. Aldate's he caught sight of Mrs. Willey's car in the spot where he had left it, thinking he would be picking it up again in a few minutes. Heaven knew how long it would remain there now, and she would have a whacking great parking fine to pay which was all his own fault. The thought of this nagged at John's mind and intermittently distracted his thoughts from his present danger. He stared gloomily at Jimmy's back and wondered whether there was any help to be had from that quarter. Could Jimmy be appealed to at any point, or would he remain a loyal agent of Sir Roderick right up to the bitter end? The old man himself sat quiet and relaxed, with his hand on the arm rest, showing no sign of strain or emotion, giving no hint of what he intended to do. No wonder the police and everybody else was taken in. John himself was beginning to find it difficult to believe in his own danger.

As they crossed Folly Bridge he asked casually where they were going, just as if this was a little social outing.

"Up Boar's Hill," was the polite reply. "We will find a quiet spot where we can talk without being disturbed. And if that becomes tedious we can always go and look at the view."

John said no more. Sir Roderick's tone of voice had been as suavely mocking as in that useless interview. The smoother he is, the worse it will be, he said to himself, and leant back against the firm soft leather and stretched his legs. This was a very different sort of vehicle from Mrs. Willey's old banger, and yet if he coveted either of them it would be the little Morris. This luxurious monster was out of his class; he had no desire to live in such a style and be an object of envy to others. He relaxed with eyes half-closed, inwardly summoning up all his resources of mind and body to face whatever was to come, and covertly assessing his two companions. If it came to a fight it would be two to one, but on the other hand they were old and he was young. But of course they might have firearms, in which case he hadn't a hope. Except that even firearms were much too crude a method for Sir Roderick. It would be much more subtle than that; something that could not possibly be traced to him. Oh, Alice, he prayed, use your wits and think up something quick.

At the very moment when Sir Roderick's Daimler was crossing Folly Bridge, Graham Price put a large cardboard box down on the doorstep of the house in Walton Terrace and felt in his pocket for his key. The door was opened before he had found it by a distraught-looking Mrs. Willey who immediately poured out an incoherent story about her car.

"But when did he take it?" asked Graham as soon as he could get a word in.

"Hours and hours ago," was the reply. "Two o'clock or half past at the very latest because that's when I got back from my friend round the corner where I'd been to lunch. And it's gone six now, and he said he wouldn't be too long. Whatever can have happened? I never knew John to do such a thing before. I don't mind a bit him using the car, because he's so very kind about it, but to take it without asking me, and for hours and hours on end."

Graham had to agree that it was both odd and rather worrying because it was so unlike John to be so inconsiderate.

"I know it is," said Mrs. Willey, "and that's why I'm so afraid he must have had an accident. He'd never have gone for so long if he could possibly help it. What's that you've got in that box?" she asked, changing the subject so abruptly that Graham was taken unawares.

"Oh. It's only something for John—or rather for some friends of his," he replied feebly.

"Friends? Not Alice Heron by any chance?"

Graham, who had not been quite sure about this before although he had had his suspicions, now became quite convinced that the autopsy on the tabby cat must indeed be connected in some way with Alice, because there was nobody else whom John would get so worked up about, except perhaps for his Victorian heroine, and a mid-twentieth-century dead cat could hardly have anything to do with her.

"Well, yes," he said slowly, recalling John's hasty manner on the telephone and the statement that a fresh crisis had arisen. Surely the only crisis for John would be something to do with Alice. "Yes," he repeated more firmly. "I wonder if I ought to take it round there. I'll have to look up the address. It's somewhere near the Parks, I think."

"Eleven Blenheim Close," said Mrs. Willey without hesitation. Addresses of people like the Herons were among the things she always managed to remember. "I'll come round with you. I'll feel awful asking if they know where John is but it won't be so bad if I've got company."

"All right," said Graham, and they walked along the quiet side roads together, and the patched-up bundle that had once been a fine tabby cat returned for the last time to its own home, its hearse a cardboard box carried by a thin, dark-haired boy in thick spectacles, its unwitting mourner a plump and puffing elderly lady.

"There's my car!" cried Mrs. Willey excitedly as they turned the corner into Blenheim Close.

But her wishes had flown ahead of her powers of perception, for when they came nearer they found that the blue Morris standing opposite the gate of Number Eleven was of a much younger vintage than Mrs. Willey's and in much better condition.

"Oh," she said in great disappointment, "and I thought everything would be all right now. Whose can it be, I wonder?"

Graham could not enlighten her. They trod the gravel

path together and stood nervously side by side at the imposing doorway. It was a relief to them both when Alice, whom they had met before, welcomed them in.

"Ah, you've brought the box," she said at once to Graham. "Just leave it here in the hall, will you? I'll deal with it later. And Mrs. Willey, I'm most dreadfully sorry about your car. It was all my fault and you must not blame John, and I'll explain all about it but there isn't time now, because Professor Woodward is here at my request and he's going to rush off to do something for me, so if you will excuse me a moment—"

"What's up? Anything new, Alice?"

The newcomer was a short, stocky man who had emerged from the drawing-room. He looked at Graham and Mrs. Willey with interest. "Do I know you? Ought I to know you?"

Alice made hasty introductions. Professor Woodward turned to Graham when she had finished and said: "You a friend of John Broome's? Want to do him a good turn? Got an hour or two to spare?"

"Sure," said Graham instantly.

"Right. We'll be off. Police station first. Keep smiling, Alice. I'm sure there'll turn out to be some innocuous explanation of the whole thing."

They all crowded to the front door, with Mrs. Willey bringing up the rear.

"The car!" shouted Alice when Sam Woodward and Graham were nearly at the gate. "Mrs. Willey's car—it'll be parked near the police station—can you drop her there? Go on, go on," she said, hustling Mrs. Willey after the men. "They'll give you a lift and you can pick it up. It'll save you a bus ride and you can drive it home."

"But I don't want to go home," gasped Mrs. Willey. "If John's in any trouble I want to help him."

"All right, argue it out between you," said Alice, "but get going now."

She shut the front door behind them and leant back against it with her eyes closed. After all the noise and movement of the last few minutes the house felt very quiet. The new nurse had not yet arrived and there was no one left in the big house except herself and the old lady lying upstairs.

She took a few deep breaths and then opened her eyes and saw the cardboard box that Graham had put down at one side of the front door, with its flaps loosely folded over the top. She knelt down and raised them slowly one by one, steeling herself to look inside. But it was not so bad after all. Graham had carried out his task with great kindness and tact. The box was full of tissue paper and only its weight and the faint greyness showing through the tissue told her that it held a grimmer content. There was even a faint smell of disinfectant, and no unpleasantness evident at all. She did not disturb the paper, but simply knelt there gripping the sides of the box, deep in thought. She was not even aware that she had spoken aloud when she muttered: "Poor old Quizzy. I wonder why."

When she heard movement and a voice speaking right beside her she came to herself with a start of alarm.

"Auntie! You ought not to be out of bed."

Lady Heron in her nightgown looked a most pitiful little bundle of skin and bones. She was bent almost double, leaning over her stick. Her breath came painfully but her eyes were very much alive, staring at the cardboard box.

"Who brought him back?" she whispered.

"John's friend. He's been very kind about it." Alice made as if to fold the flaps over again but Lady Heron staggered forward and took one hand off her stick to point at the box as she cried out loudly. "Stop! Leave it!"

"Oh, Auntie," said Alice, getting to her feet and putting an arm round the old woman. "Do you really have to look at him?"

"Yes, I do," she cried. "You wouldn't understand. You're young and pretty and for all your troubles you've always had people to love you and you always will. I haven't and I never will. I've only had Quizzy. Yes, I do have to look at him but you needn't if you don't want to. I won't be long. Help me to kneel down."

Alice did as she was told and held an arm round the quivering little body to steady it and turned her own face away. Her eyes were brimming and she could not speak.

"All right," said Lady Heron firmly. "I've covered him up. You can look round now. Help me up, please, and help me back to bed. And dispose of the box in any way you think fit. I shall not wish to see or hear of him again."

They moved slowly upstairs together, Alice choking down tears, her aunt dry-eyed. When Lady Heron was once more relaxed against the pillows Alice leant over and kissed her and said: "It's not true, what you said just now. I love you very much. And John cares for you too."

The rigid face softened a little. "He's not a bad boy."

"Oh, Auntie Belle!" It was Alice's turn to need comfort. "What's going to happen? Where are they now? Did I do right to send for Professor Woodward and tell him everything?"

"You did perfectly right and he will do all he can. You and I alone could have done nothing. We must hope—hope—hope . . ."

Her voice faded away and her eyes closed. For a moment Alice feared that her heart had stopped beating, that the excitement of the day and the effort of coming down to say farewell to Quizzy had been too great a strain, but the pulse was fairly steady and the light breathing was even. Lady Heron had simply collapsed suddenly into an exhausted sleep. Alice moved over to the low chair near the window and slumped down on it and closed her eyes too.

13

Jimmy turned the Daimler off the quiet lane into the entrance of a field of rough pasture. The rain was coming down heavily again and it mingled with the water dripping from the overhanging trees to beat a ceaseless tattoo on the roof of the car. With the windscreen wipers switched off the glass soon misted over and there was very little to be seen of the outside world.

"I do not think anyone is likely to disturb us here for a little while," said Sir Roderick placidly. "This field is normally occupied by a fine Jersey herd, I believe, but they will have been called in for milking by now."

John made no response. He was much too occupied in trying to keep his head and in watching the other's movements to have any energy left for making small talk about cows.

"Cigarette?" said Sir Roderick, offering a gold case. John shook his head. "Jimmy?"

Jimmy turned round and accepted one and the two old

139

men lit up and puffed contentedly in silence for a few moments, while John wondered if he was to be subjected to torture by suspense.

"What do you want most out of life, John?" asked Sir Roderick presently in a friendly way.

It was absolutely impossible not to make some sort of answer.

"To do well in the line I've chosen and not to injure anybody, I suppose," muttered John.

"Two very worthy aims that may unfortunately come into conflict with each other," commented Sir Roderick. "The chosen line being presumably something to do with literature. You wish to write yourself? You have literary ambitions?"

"Yes," said John in an agony of discomfort and apprehension. He hated talking about his secret ambitions at the best of times and even to a sympathetic audience, because it seemed so platitudinous for a student of literature to want to be a writer himself. He was terribly afraid of failure and would rather pretend that he had no such ambitions than be seen to fail in them.

And yet here he was, being metaphorically prodded in his most tender spots instead of being physically attacked as he had expected. If they were going to shoot him then for God's sake why didn't they get on with it? How long was he going to have to sit out this ghastly farce? Should he get out of the car and run? Or was that what they were playing for, so that they could switch on the engine and run him down, here in this lonely spot, with no other witness near?

Yet another road accident due to the carelessness of a pedestrian. "He shot straight out on to the road in front of me, sir," Jimmy would say to the magistrates, and his evidence would be unquestioningly accepted with all the weight of Sir Roderick's authority to back it up. Another murder in the true Heron style. He felt sure that this was what was going to happen, and yet it was not primarily fear that held him back from the jump, but an absurd feeling of embarrassment. It would look so awfully silly to behave like that when somebody was only making polite enquiries about your future career.

"And you no doubt have much greater sensitivity than the average," went on Sir Roderick, "and a much more vivid imagination. A writer's imagination."

"I don't know," said John with a fresh uneasiness. It was not so much physical fear now; it was not even the fear of making a fool of himself. It was more like the cold, shrinking certainty of the weaker party in a vital match, who feels himself being outplayed and manoeuvred slowly but inexorably into defeat, without any hope of preventing it but condemned to fight hopelessly back until the very end.

"I believe you have a very vivid imagination indeed," Sir Roderick said, "particularly when both your feelings and your intellectual curiosity are aroused. I do not pretend to be a literary critic, as I said before, but it would not surprise me at all if you did not turn out some good imaginative writing one day—novels most likely, or even some sort of poetic fantasy. You need to mature first, of course, and bring balance and order into your imagination, and it may well take some time before you start to produce really good work. I shall probably not live to see it, although I reckon I am good for another ten years yet, and a lot can happen to a young man in the ten years between twenty-two and thirty-two. You are twenty-two, aren't you, John?"

"Yes," said John. He felt as if he was on the verge of losing his mental balance completely, of toppling over into a world where nothing was what it seemed, a fantastic world where black was white and white was black, where things changed their nature in front of your very eyes,

dissolved as you touched them. He tried to tell himself that
the old man was trying to bribe him, not crudely with offers
of money or even with offers of Alice, but so subtly and
flatteringly, and above all, so interestingly, that it was
almost impossible to resist it. But he would have to resist it;
he was in mortal danger, not perhaps of being shot or run
over, but of being brainwashed into losing all judgement of
his own, of becoming the sort of unquestioning puppet of
Sir Roderick that Jimmy, sitting silently in front of them,
appeared to be.

The old man talked on. Against his will John began to
thaw and respond. It is all an act, he said to himself
desperately. But if it was, it was the most convincing act
that he had ever seen or could ever imagine seeing, either in
the theatre or out of it. Not only that, but it was a real
give-and-take discussion, an intellectual pleasure of a rare
order; more interesting even than exchanging ideas with his
academic superiors, for here was a first-class mind that was
not tied down to any techniques or theories of its own.

"It must be a very frightening experience for the writer or
artist," said Sir Roderick after John had been giving his
views on the imaginative reality of a novel as opposed to the
reality experienced in daily life, "a very frightening experience indeed to feel the borderline dissolving, as it were.
An Alice in Wonderland sort of experience, if I may use a
suitable Oxford example. I have always thought the Alice
books very frightening to the adult mind, haven't you? A
total acceptance of the fantasy world is not, of course, usual
even among imaginative writers—they would presumably
all be in lunatic asylums if it were—but a powerful imagination will work even upon the ordinary little realities of
daily life and create a fiction out of them which still has
its own sort of validity. You would agree with me there,
John?"

"Yes, I would agree," said John, but with less warmth and enthusiasm than he had displayed during the last few minutes of their conversation. That part of his mind that had not been wholly seduced had an inkling now of where it was being led. He stared at the back of Jimmy's head and waited.

"In many cases," went on Sir Roderick, " this is fairly harmless. We all have our day-dreams, we all spin stories about ourselves and our neighbours. It doesn't matter so long as we don't act on them, so long as we retain enough sense of the daily life reality not to allow the fantastic superstructure to get out of hand. Don't you agree?"

"Yes," said John, feeling once more the helpless floating sensation, as if he was being driven along by an irresistible force of nature, by the winds or by the tides.

"But if we do allow them to get out of hand to such a degree that they take control of our daily lives, then we are in danger of causing a lot of harm. Gossip and scandal can be very unpleasant things. The true creative mind should be above such crudenesses. If it stoops to them then it can fall into the danger I have mentioned. It can find that the borderline between fantasy and reality is dissolving. It can build up a great edifice of fantasy and become so attached to this, its precious brain-child, that it cannot let it go, and it will start trying to twist reality to fit its dream. You are much too intelligent, John," and here the old man turned round and displayed his warmest and most benevolent smile, "not to know exactly what I am talking about. You will understand that I have seen you yourself fall into just this danger and that I have brought you up here to help you regain your normal balance and dispel this fantasy world before it is too late, before you take some action that you will afterwards regret. You do appreciate that, don't you?"

"Yes," said John hopelessly. He could struggle no more.

The old man was right. He had created his own version of Emily Witherington's death; he had created his own version of more recent events. There was not a scrap of real evidence that Sir Roderick had killed Emily. Even those vital last letters could have lots of perfectly innocent interpretations. While as for Letty Mann, what had he to go on except the fact that she had stolen the letters from him and that he had fished out of the river a hat that looked rather like one of hers?

"Letty Mann," said Sir Roderick gently as if reading John's thoughts, "was very impertinent this morning, as these apparently humble creatures sometimes are, and I was obliged to reprimand her quite severely. She left the house in a huff, without even cooking the lunch. We were all rather anxious about her and, as you heard me explain at the police station, Jimmy and I drove around for a while trying to find her. When this call came from her friend—Mrs. Fairfield I believe the name was—our minds were of course put at rest, but we were then worried about you. You do not imagine, I trust," he went on, looking at John with great concern, "that this telephone call is only a part of my own fantasy?"

"No," said John, "I believe you."

And he did. He had no reason whatever to disbelieve it, any more than the police sergeant had had. But it was not only Letty, he thought confusedly; it was Lady Heron too. She had backed him up in his notion that Sir Roderick was a murderer; she had encouraged him to go on believing it. And she was not a romantic day-dreamer like Letty or a blundering fool like John himself. She had been in it from the first; she was very shrewd, and she knew everything.

"But Lady Heron," he said aloud.

"Oh dear." Sir Roderick sounded really distressed. "I was afraid you would mention my wife and place me in a cruel dilemma. You are suggesting, no doubt, that this fantastic tale that you have built up in your mind was supported by so-called evidence adduced by my wife?"

John nodded.

"Ah, I see it all now," said Sir Roderick softly. "It is only too grievously plain. Poor Belle. She has not had a happy life, though many no doubt would consider it enviable. Poor Belle. I see how the misunderstanding has come about, and I would add to what I said just now. I would guess that your fantasy was not only supported by my wife but was actually triggered off by her in the first place. You had none of these strange ideas in your mind until Lady Heron suggested the matter?"

"No," admitted John, "I had none of them until then."

"And never would have. Poor Belle. What trouble she has caused. What vindictiveness can reside even in the breast of an old woman nearing the end of her days. One would have expected her to have come to terms with it by now, but apparently not. Jealousy is not only a very destructive emotion, but an extraordinarily persistent one. Even jealousy of the dead."

"Jealousy of the dead," echoed John. It awoke an echo in his mind, that particular phrase. What was it that Alice had once said, not so very long ago, though it seemed now as if it had been in another life? He had been boring her as usual about Emily Witherington. "Oh well," she had said, "I suppose it's better to have a glamorous dead lady as a rival than a glamorous living one." He had been just a trifle offended for a split second, and then they had laughed together and been very happy.

But Lady Heron's jealousy had not been so easily dispersed. After all, it had not been the dead but the living Emily who was her rival. And her successful rival, in Sir Roderick's heart at least, if not in the eyes of the world.

Lady Heron had lived long with her own bitterness; John had recognized that very early on. And she had actually asked him, not merely by innuendo, but quite openly, to take revenge upon her husband because she was not capable of doing it herself.

Oh, it was true, true, true! Everything Sir Roderick was saying was true, and he, John, had simply been staring at the wrong side of the coin all along, having all the evidence in front of him but putting the wrong interpretation on it.

"You will not wish me to go very much farther into this very delicate and distressing matter, I am sure," said Sir Roderick. "My wife is ailing and cannot have very much longer in this world. You would not wish to darken her last little time on earth?"

Again John shook his head. Suddenly an odd and seemingly quite irrelevant scrap of information came into his mind and in his helpless confusion he spoke it aloud.

"She was a Molyneux, wasn't she? Daughter of the *Foundations of Perception* Molyneux?"

"Yes indeed, and a considerable scholar in her own right." Sir Roderick paused a moment. "You have gathered, I suppose, from your researches," he went on softly, "that she was the Miss Isabella Molyneux who gave evidence at the enquiry into Miss Witherington's death? That she was the first to come upon the fatality and to examine the body for signs of life? You do realize that? Or perhaps you do not," continued Sir Roderick as John, who felt a great wave of nausea and a difficulty in speaking, failed to respond. "No, you would not know all this. I was forgetting. The fact that she was first on the scene was kept out of the papers—no doubt through her father's influence. You will only have read the published record."

"Yes," said John. He could see himself now, sitting at the table in his basement room, going over the accounts of

Emily's death in the hope of pinning the responsibility firmly on to Sir Roderick. He could see himself reluctantly connecting the girl witness with the Lady Heron of sixty years later, and he could see himself deliberately leaving that piece of information out of his summary. He had committed the unforgivable sin of any investigator or research worker: failed to follow up an obvious lead because it might conflict with his own deeply-held theory. He had excused himself by saying that Lady Heron must be innocent or she would never have sought his help, but in his heart he knew that it was because he wanted to believe Sir Roderick guilty. Partly out of pity for Lady Heron, but partly because Sir Roderick had deeply hurt John's own self-respect and all his pride was crying out for revenge.

It seemed to him now that he had been the victim of them both, the old man and the old woman alike. They had destroyed him between them, yes, and Alice had played her part too. They had all been entertaining themselves with the charming little game of playing shuttlecock with the heart and mind of John Broome. His thoughts were a fog of confusion; truth was a quicksand.

And yet somewhere behind it all there was a little spot of firm ground, a little shred of genuine reasoning; he knew it was there and he tried to catch hold of it as a drowning man catches at a straw. It was something to do with the cat. It slipped out of his grasp and he was back in the morass.

"I think," said Sir Roderick, "that I had better say no more. I beg you will never refer to this again for my wife's sake. Now let us forget that this conversation ever took place and revert to the *status quo ante*. It appears to have stopped raining at last, and Jimmy has had a good long sleep. We will drive round and take a peep at the famous view before going home. If Letty has returned to her duties perhaps you will take a light supper with us, since it is too late to enjoy our normal dinner now, I fear. If she is still sulking out at Cowley, then no doubt Alice will rustle us up something, as the saying goes."

The big car reversed into the country lane. They drove slowly along to near the place where the best view of Oxford was to be had. Jimmy remained in his seat, but John got out at Sir Roderick's suggestion and went with him to gaze upon the distant dreaming spires, glowing now in the evening light, enticing yet unreachable, like a mirage in the desert or a vision from another world.

Had anything really happened to him at all? Was his whole life in Oxford just a dream? Was Sir Roderick part of the dream too?

He glanced sideways at the old man. The profile was firm and motionless. There was not a hint of any sort of feeling upon that icy marble face. It was inhuman; it surely could not be real.

"The new ring-road system," said Sir Roderick pointing with his stick, "is going to have the effect rather of a medieval moat or a city wall, isolating the city from the outside world, and making of it something of a museum-piece rather than a living community. Don't you agree?"

They returned to the car, talking peaceably about the rape of the countryside. They might have been out for a pleasant evening stroll. But when they were once more in the car and Sir Roderick's flow seemed for a moment to have come to a halt, that little shred of reasoning that had been eluding John came at last within his grasp.

"What about the cat?" he blurted out.

"The cat?" The old man appeared nonplussed. "What cat?"

"Quizzy. He's dead."

"Oh yes. Poor old Quizzy. That wasn't quite up to your usual standard, John." Sir Roderick shook his head reproachfully. "All that cloak-and-dagger stuff—bearing off the corpse in the darkness of the night. Too melodramatic, my dear fellow. That's something you will have to guard against when you compose your fictions."

"But he had been poisoned," persisted John.

"Very possibly. I believe I mentioned the danger myself."

"He had not been eating grass treated with weed-killer," said John. "He'd been poisoned in his dinner."

He held on to the memory of that limp little body as to the only sure thing in a spinning world. Whatever else was true or not true, Lady Heron had not poisoned her cat. And the very thought of Quizzy roused him to a fury that nothing could subdue, not all the force of the old man's eloquence and the paralysing effect that it was having upon John's mind.

"And how," asked Sir Roderick, "were you enabled to come to such a conclusion? I am somewhat taken aback, I admit, to learn that you include a knowledge of pathology among your accomplishments."

"I got the stomach contents analysed," muttered John.

"Really? By whom? The public analyst? I must admit to yet more ignorance. I did not realize than an autopsy on a cat was part of his official duties."

"It isn't. Not as far as I know."

"Then who, may I enquire, carried out the investigation?"

"Friend of mine," said John miserably, seeing no other way out, but knowing only too well where this was going to lead and wincing, in spite of himself, under the mockery in the old man's voice.

"A friend in high places, no doubt."

"No," said John. There was a silence. Sir Roderick simply waited. "As a matter of fact it was a chemistry student I know," said John at last, as he had known he was going to do.

"Oh." The eyebrows shot up and there were volumes of polite scepticism contained in the one monosyllable.

John said no more. The effort of trying to get a foot-hold on his own sense of reality had exhausted him.

While they were held up in the stream of traffic queueing to cross the narrow bridge, a blue Morris Minor shot out of its lane and drew up alongside them, to the accompaniment of angry hootings from behind. John, seated on the offside of the Daimler, looked up at it and after a moment of blankness recognized three familiar faces inside, two male and one female.

"Good God," he exclaimed.

But his astonishment was nothing compared to that on those three faces.

"Where've you been?" yelled Graham, winding down the window of the seat next to the driver.

Instinctively John returned to Sir Roderick for instructions before replying. The old man smiled at him encouragingly, leaned across him, and said: "Do I detect Professor Woodward at the wheel?"

The driver of the other car smiled back. "Yes, sir, you do."

The frantic hooting drowned all further words; the traffic was moving on, and the two cars were blocking the way. Sir Roderick signed to Jimmy to let the Morris slip in front of the Daimler, since it was straddled on to the wrong side of the road and had no other chance of returning to its proper lane. Professor Woodward acknowledged the courtesy by raising a hand, and drove on, with Graham's head poking out of the window beaming at John, and Mrs. Willey's face visible through the back window, smiling equally happily.

"What are they all looking so pleased about?" John asked himself dully. "Did they think I'd vanished for ever?"

14

Graham drew his head in from the window as the Morris pulled ahead of the Daimler. "Thank God he's all right," he said.

"Thank God," echoed Mrs. Willey from the back seat.

"It's a very great relief, I must say," said Professor Woodward in rather more moderate terms. He was looking extremely thoughtful as he edged the car through the traffic.

"It looks as if they'd just gone out for a ride," said Graham.

"I wonder," said Professor Woodward, neatly nipping in front of a lorry, "whether we aren't the ones who have been taken for a ride."

"What do you mean?"

"How well do you know John, both of you?" countered the Professor. "What, for instance, would you say matters to him more than anything else in the world?"

"Alice," said Mrs. Willey with no hesitation at all.

"And you, Graham?"

152

"Well—er—yes, I suppose so. Alice." said Graham with a certain amount of embarrassment.

"Matters enough to him to make him lose his head a little?"

"Oh yes," cried Mrs. Willey. "He's quite lost his head over her. She's such a very sweet girl."

"I didn't quite mean that," said the Professor, "although you are no doubt right. What do you think, Graham? You know what I mean, don't you?"

"I think I can guess," said Graham, looking rather uncomfortable, "but actually I don't know John all that well. I mean I like him a lot and we get on fine but I haven't a clue what really makes him tick. I mean I'm only a chemist and I don't understand a literary person like John."

"In what way?" Sam Woodward pressed him for an answer. They were yet again held up in the traffic.

"Well, he's got a very vivid imagination for one thing. And he seems to get very worked up about his theories. I mean his theories about the people he's researching into. I sometimes think they are almost more real to him than the actual people around him, if you see what I mean, and he doesn't always notice things about the actual people that are quite obvious. At least they seem obvious to me," amended Graham.

"That's a very interesting observation you have made," said Professor Woodward. "Let us give thanks for the scientific mind."

They moved on again, to the accompaniment of an outburst from Mrs. Willey in defence of John, whom she vaguely understood was being criticized, although she did not quite understand why.

"Well, we shall see," said the Professor. "I look forward to having a talk with John myself, but meanwhile the first priority is to get back to Blenheim Close and reassure Alice.

Unless they overtake us and get there first, which they don't look like doing. I can't see any sign of the Daimler," he added, glancing in the mirror.

"Stuck behind that lorry probably," said Graham. "It's such a size."

"Ah, that's where we gain, we humble folk with our trusty little nippers," said the Professor, giving an affectionate pat to the steering-wheel, and the remaining minutes of the drive were taken up by a dialogue between himself and Mrs. Willey in praise of the Morris.

Alice, watching from the drawing-room window, saw the car arrive and rushed out of the house to meet them. Professor Woodward gave her an encouraging wave and a smile as he came towards her.

"All is well. They are following some way behind—your uncle and John. Both very much alive and kicking and on excellent terms with each other."

"Thank God for that!" cried Alice fervently. She caught sight of Graham and Mrs. Willey hovering uncertainly near the gate. "Would you like to come in and have a drink?" she said. "And let me thank you properly?"

They thought not; it was time they got on with their own affairs, and there was still Mrs. Willey's car to be collected from near the police station. Graham offered to accompany her to it and they departed together.

"But what had happened?" asked Alice as she returned to the house with Professor Woodward.

"I don't know." His face was very serious as he explained the meeting of the two cars. "I shall be interested to learn the full story," he added.

"I do hope they really are coming back," said Alice, quick to take alarm again.

"I have not the least doubt of it," said the Professor with great confidence. "What is worrying me is something quite different. You told me how you discovered John's belief that your uncle was implicated in the death of a certain lady sixty years ago. Had you ever had any suspicion of this yourself before today?"

"Not the slightest."

"And your aunt? Had she ever given any hint?"

"I've never heard her mention anything."

"Nor anyone else among your friends and relations?"

"None, none," cried Alice. "I told you. It was a dreadful shock to me, even then, even after realizing that Uncle had—I mean, even after—"

She stopped in confusion.

"Alice," said Professor Woodward sternly. "There's something important that you've been keeping back from me."

"It's only something rather beastly," she said, recovering herself, "that I'd rather not tell you if you don't mind. It's nothing to do with the Emily Witherington business, honestly. It's just that Uncle and Auntie have quarrelled all their lives and taken it out on each other in rather nasty ways and this was particularly nasty."

"H'm," said the Professor, "I would rather have had all the facts. However. Let's get back to the main problem. When you found these notes that John had been making you had no doubt at all that he was correct in his assumptions?"

"None," said Alice in a very low voice. And then she added firmly: "John would never think ill of anyone without very good reason and he would never tell a lie."

"I agree with you. I have the highest opinion of John's character. And of his intelligence. But he might still have made a mistake. Even the best of us can do that. He might well have drawn the wrong conclusions from his evidence, as many people have done before him and will do again, both in the law courts and in scholarship."

"Oh, if only that were true!" cried Alice.

"I think it is not impossible," said the Professor gently. "There's just one more thing. You answered the telephone when the police rang to say John was there with Miss Mann's hat, and you thought yourself that meant that Miss Mann was dead?"

"Yes, at that moment I did," said Alice.

"And then your uncle took over the phone and told the police he had had a call from a friend of Miss Mann's through a coin-box?"

Alice nodded.

"Did you actually hear that call?"

She shook her head. "But I was upstairs with Auntie. I might not have heard."

Professor Woodward screwed up his face. "It's a pity you can't vouch for it. Did you know Miss Mann had such a friend?"

Again Alice shook her head.

"Did your aunt know?"

"I suppose I could ask her," said Alice doubtfully.

"Never mind," said Professor Woodward, who had walked over to the window. "It's too late now. Here they are. It won't be long to wait now until we know the truth. Meanwhile no indiscretions, mind. Take your cue from your uncle."

Sir Roderick was radiating geniality as he came into the house.

"Spot of trouble with the car," he said. "That's why we've been so long. Jimmy's working on it now. He'll be in presently for a bite to eat. Letty not back yet?"

"No, Uncle." Alice kissed him. "Hullo, John," she said brightly. "You must be hungry. I'll get you some supper. What about you, Uncle Rod?"

"Well, if you really don't mind, my love," said Sir Roderick consulting his watch. "I think that would be preferable to waiting for Letty. John here is ravenous and I'm getting a bit peckish myself. You'll join us, Woodward? Just a very simple cold meal, I fear, though I must say this for Alice—she makes a very good salad dressing. Meanwhile we can at least slake our thirst."

He shepherded Professor Woodward into the drawing-room. John, who had not spoken yet, caught Alice's eye and instinctively took a step forward to follow her into the kitchen. Sir Roderick glanced round. "John, you will join us?"

It was a command rather than a question. John followed the two older men into the drawing-room. He seemed no longer to have any will of his own. Even the sight of Alice's smiling face had brought no comfort, because she too seemed to belong to this nightmarish Through-the-Looking-Glass world, where everything was the wrong way round, and he knew it was, but he hardly knew how to hold on to his own sanity, let alone prove to anyone else that he was the only one who was sane.

He drank his whisky, which tasted real enough, and listened to the conversation of the other two. They were talking about Oxford's traffic problems and the attempts to solve them. Just what one might expect when two old Oxford residents got together. It was a subject that was on everybody's mind at the moment. Nothing could be more normal and natural, more utterly rooted in that reality of daily life that Sir Roderick was so fond of talking about. Every now and then one of them politely deferred to him, and he made appropriate replies.

How did Sam Woodward get here, he wondered vaguely at one point, and was trying to summon up the strength to ask him when Sir Roderick once more jumped in first, with his uncanny instinct for the least hint of rebellious feelings in John.

"Good to see you again, Woodward," he said, slipping the remark neatly into a slight pause in the conversation. "Alice asked you along, did she? Or were you just passing by?"

"Alice phoned me," was the reply. "She was a little anxious and wanted to be reassured." The Professor's eyes twinkled as he looked from Sir Roderick to John and then back again. "Seemed to think there was some sort of misunderstanding had arisen between the two of you— wanted me to try to resolve it. Hence that somewhat melodramatic car chase just now."

He made a humorously deprecating face at his host, who responded in like manner. It was as if they were saying to each other: these women, with their fears and fancies, got to humour them.

Professor Woodward appeared to be well entrenched in the Looking-Glass world too. No help to be had from there. What about Alice herself? Was there any chance at all that she would live up to the unshakably realistic standards of her famous namesake? John feared not. She would be only too relieved to have all suspicions removed from her beloved uncle. She would gladly stay in the world of pretence for ever if it meant that dear Uncle Rod was safe. And Jimmy was a helpless tool, and Letty, poor silly day-dreaming Letty, whose attempt to compensate for the humiliations of her own wretched little life had started it all off in the first place, Letty was dead. That little bit of John's mind that was still fighting hard for independence knew with certainty that Letty was dead. He did not for one moment believe in that phone call. But it was of no help now; it would be discovered in due course, and it would no doubt be neatly fitted into the fabric of the pretence world too.

There was no hope at all. Or rather, there was only one. A little crippled old woman now lying asleep upstairs. An indomitable spirit housed in a feeble, failing body. She might or might not have killed Emily, but she could not possibly have pushed Letty into the river and she most certainly had not poisoned her cat.

What would Lady Heron do when she awoke and found her husband triumphantly manipulating them all? Would she submit to being part of the pretence world too? Would she play the role assigned to her by her husband, who would no doubt now treat her with the exaggerated consideration and pity that he had displayed when speaking of her to John during their talk on Boar's Hill? She must know that her life would be worth nothing even if she did give in and play his game; she would be too great a threat; in a very short while he would dispose of her too.

But then her life was worth very little to her in any case, loveless and full of pain. Unlike her husband, who at eighty could still look forward to ten years of good health in which to dominate others and rule his own little corner of the world. She might well try to fight, thought John as he accepted another drink and made a suitable reply to Sir Roderick's favourite question, "Do you agree?"

The trouble was that Lady Heron's lonely fight could not add up to much. She had nothing left but her brains and her determination. There was no other strength left in her. She was shrunken so much that even Alice could lift her without difficulty. What could she do against the combined forces of her husband and the rest of the world? And John, whom she had trusted, had failed her completely. He felt hopeless,

utterly beaten down and also bitterly ashamed as he followed the others out of the room in response to Alice's call
that supper was ready. They stood for a moment near the
foot of the stairs, the three of them, and Alice joined them.

"If you'd like to go into the dining-room," she said, "I'll
just take Auntie's tray up first."

John, closely watching Sir Roderick, saw his features
compose themselves into suitable lines for an expression of
concern for the comfort and well-being of his wife, but only
half of it was ever uttered. It was interrupted by a shrill cry
from the floor above. Four faces looked up to see a tiny
little figure in a long white nightgown leaning against the
rail that encircled the first-floor landing. Only the head and
arms appeared above the rail and one arm was stretched out
gripping a solid oak stick.

"So you're back!" she screamed. "You murdering black-
hearted villain! You killed him! You killed my Quizzy!"

There was a split second of shocked silence before Sir
Roderick found his voice.

"My dear Belle," he began, looking up at her.

They were the last words he spoke. The other three, as if
by a common instinct of self-preservation, jumped back as
the stick flew out of her hand. In their instinctive concern
for their own safety, and in the total unexpectedness and
suddenness of it all, not one of the three was able afterwards
to say exactly what happened. Had she let go of the stick
intentionally or had it slipped from her crippled hand? And
did it hit Sir Roderick's upturned face before he began to
stagger or after he had already started to fall?

At the time of the happening these questions were not
asked, for there was too much to be done in summoning
medical help and getting Lady Heron, unconscious but still
breathing, back into bed, and her husband on to the
drawing-room sofa, where he was soon after pronounced by

Dr. Lethbridge to have suffered a fatal coronary attack, probably on account of some extra strain that was too much for even his splendid health to withstand.

"It's a good way to go, my dear," he said to the white-faced Alice. "A terrible shock for you, but best for him. He would have wished it to be that way. He would have hated to become sick and feeble and unable to get around and carry on his usual activities."

"That bruise on the temple." It was Professor Woodward who spoke. John had his arm round Alice. He dared not speak to her; he had no idea how she was going to behave towards him now. It was enough for the moment that she did not repulse him when he made this gesture of comfort.

"Nothing to do with it," said the doctor promptly. "Hit something as he fell most likely. Could have been the knob at the bottom of the banisters. Did none of you see?"

They all shook their heads, moved yet again by an instinct common to them all. Lady Heron's stick lay in the shadows under the hall table. There was no reason why the doctor should notice it; in any case there was no reason why it should not be lying there.

"Well, it really doesn't matter," said Dr. Lethbridge. "There is no doubt about the cause of death. We must think of your aunt now, my dear." He turned to Alice. "The new nurse will be more congenial to you than the other. I am sorry you had that trouble with her. I will sit by your aunt myself until she arrives."

"Will she get better?" Alice asked.

"We must go on hoping," said the doctor, but John did not derive much hope from his expression. "She has some reserves of strength still left, I believe."

Lady Heron had indeed some strength left in reserve, but very little. She rallied enough later in the evening to listen impassively while Alice and the doctor between them told her of her husband's death, and then she sank into a coma from which it seemed scarcely possible that she could recover.

15

Meanwhile Letty did not come home. The next morning, at Professor Woodward's instigation, a police search was carried out. The body was found caught up in water-weeds and roots of trees, some way downstream from the spot where John had found the hat. It was fully clothed and there was no sign of any injury. Nor was there any sign of the black handbag. The same sergeant who had listened so sceptically to John's story at the police station, brought the news to Alice.

"Mr. Broome is staying here with us now, if you want to speak to him," she said. She went upstairs to where John sat by the unconscious old woman's side. The quiet, pleasant little nurse tactfully left the room. Alice told John the news and after she had finished her eyes pleaded with him.

"I know nothing of how Letty died," he said with a calm determination more reassuring than any amount of eager protestations would have been. "I have no evidence that anyone might have wished to take her life. I went to seek

163

her at the request of your aunt and yourself, in a place where she was sometimes known to walk, and I found what I believed to be her hat floating in the river. That is all I know. That is what I shall tell the police."

Her eyes thanked him. The sergeant, who was waiting below in the big drawing-room, spoke to him with all the deference due to a young man who looked completely at home and at his ease in this luxurious house, and actually called John "Sir."

Jimmy, whose turn came next, received less deferential treatment. His statement that Sir Roderick had told him to drive around the streets of East Oxford looking for Miss Mann was examined in some detail.

"Who decided where you should go?" asked the sergeant.

"The guv'nor, of course," was the curt reply.

"And you didn't stop at all? To plan where to look next, perhaps?"

"Of course we stopped. Several times."

"Where?"

Jimmy mentioned several spots. The sergeant pounced on the last one. "Off St. Clements? That'd be only a short walk from where Miss Mann was found drowned in the river," he said meaningly.

Jimmy said nothing.

"Did you get out of the car?"

"No."

"Sir Roderick didn't ask you to get out and do any little errand for him—buy him some cigarettes, for example?"

This statement did evoke some response in the surly little old man, but the emotion he displayed was indignation, not fear or guilt.

"In the mucky little tobacconist's round there!" he exclaimed. "As if the guv'nor would've bought his fags from a place like that! Didn't even get 'em in Oxford. Had 'em sent down every month from London. Picadilly."

The bleary old eyes rested contemptuously on the interrogator for a moment, and then Jimmy turned away, blinking as if his eyes were hurting him.

It was then suggested that he, as an old retainer, might have been jealous of the lady companion who held such a privileged position in the household, but at this Jimmy merely stared. Nothing could shake him in any part of his statement, and any suspicion that he might have had a hand in Letty's death soon petered out in the total lack of any evidence.

Nobody had been walking along by the river on that damp and chilly afternoon; no witness of Letty's death was to be found, and nobody mourned her passing. The nearest relative, a cousin who lived in South London, seemed concerned only to establish that it could not have been suicide, and was satisfied when reassured on that score. A very short paragraph in the local paper sufficed to cover her death, while the national Press carried long eulogistic obituaries of Sir Roderick. Only in the minds of a very few people was any connection made between the two.

Professor Woodward was one of these few.

"Wouldn't say it in front of Alice, of course," he remarked to John in the drawing-room at Blenheim Close while Alice was out in the kitchen making yet another pot of tea, "but I thought you might like to know that I'm beginning to think you could be right after all about the way Emily Witherington died. Unscrupulous old blighter. I wouldn't put it past him to knock off a woman who was making a nuisance of herself."

He took out his pipe and waited for John to reply. John said nothing.

"Mind you, as regards this other business . . ." Professor Woodward prodded at his pipe, seemingly rather surprised that John was not taking up his invitation to discuss the whole matter. "A verdict of accidental death will no doubt be returned, which is best for all concerned, perhaps."

"Yes," agreed John.

The Professor looked at him keenly above the bowl of his pipe. "Very steep bank along that stretch of river. Grass gets very slippery when wet."

"Yes," said John again.

"And the poor woman might have been attracted by something floating in the water, just as you were. Or perhaps she wanted to look at a bird's nest, and climbed down to investigate. And slipped and was unable to save herself."

This time John made no reply.

"No earthly chance of proving anything to the contrary unless someone actually saw him . . ." The Professor broke off and gave a little cough. "Ah, well. You are quite right to be discreet."

"Yes," said John.

Sam Woodward puffed away in silence for a minute or two, while John wandered restlessly about the room. Then he came and stood in front of the older man and said very quickly, as if it were a disagreeable task that he wanted to put behind him as soon as possible: "Would you mind if I pass my notes on Emily to somebody else to write up into a book? I'm not trying to shirk it and I don't want to let you down, but I think someone else would make a better job of it now."

"But, my dear boy, it's your future career. You'll have to suppress a lot, of course, but I can advise you what you should leave out. There'll still be enough for a respectable piece of scholarship."

"I'd rather drop the whole thing," said John.

Sam Woodward looked up and caught the expression on his face. "All right," he said. "I understand. It's a great pity, but I understand. I'll fix up for you to help the editor of the new annotated Tennyson for the rest of your year in Oxford. It's a vast job, and he could do with someone like you."

John thanked him warmly, but later, when he and Alice were alone together, she listened with increasing distress to his calm announcement of his change of plan.

"If only that day we drove up Boar's Hill, I'd never suggested . . ." Her voice tailed away.

"That I should meet your uncle? I pushed you into it, didn't I? Let's cut out this 'if only' game. There's no point in it."

"But it's spoilt your chances. What's the use of being one among dozens of people working on Tennyson? You won't even be acknowledged in the preface, let alone have your name on the title page."

"Never mind." He put an arm around her and gave her a little friendly shake. "There's plenty of other books for me to write one day."

It seemed to John that his whole life now consisted of comforting people and taking decisions for them. The doctor and the police asked for him by name when they had enquiries to make or information to impart; the nurse reported on the condition of her patient to him; even Sam Woodward appeared to be bowing to his judgement, while Alice, coping with a rush of telephone calls and condolence letters about her uncle's death, sought John's help and advice at every turn.

He attended to everything as best he could, and even managed to make a suitable congratulatory speech to the new Sir Lionel.

On the afternoon of the second day after Sir Roderick's death, the old gardener, who had been pottering in and out of the house in an unhappy, bewildered way since his master died, came up to John and begged to be given some orders to carry out. Nothing would soothe him but that John should walk down the garden with him and tell him what job he ought to be getting on with next. Knowing nothing whatever about it, John said firmly that the hedge needed trimming and he would like Jimmy to do that first.

And after that, he could dig a proper grave in which to bury that old cardboard box and its contents, that had stood for two days neglected in the garden shed. It was to be a really nice little job, mind, not just throwing the earth about anyhow; and please would Jimmy plant some suitable flowers on top and find a good bit of smooth stone to mark the spot. That would please Lady Heron for sure if she ever recovered enough to be told; that was what Sir Roderick would have wished.

John left Jimmy working away contentedly and returned to the house to be met by Alice saying that her aunt had recovered consciousness and was asking to speak to John. Again her eyes appealed to him. He patted her shoulder and went upstairs.

"Would you mind waiting in the back room?" he said to the nurse. "I'll call you if she needs anything. I don't expect we shall be very long."

He came into the bedroom and took his usual seat by her side. Her hand was fumbling over the yellow bedspread and he laid his own very gently upon it. Her eyes flickered open and then the lids drooped again as if the effort of holding them up was beyond her strength. Her hand escaped from John's and wandered over the bedspread, searching.

"We buried him, said John softly. "And gave him a tombstone and some flowers for remembrance. I won't forget him. I'll always remember old Quizzy as long as I live."

Her lips moved noiselessly; her eyes opened again and thanked him.

"Take your time," said John. "There's no hurry. I'm here and I won't go away."

Her head moved sideways as if she wanted something from that direction. John picked up a glass of orange juice from the bedside table and held it to her lips. She drank eagerly, reminding him for a fleeting moment of Lady Heron as he had first seen her, biting greedily into a cucumber sandwich.

"That's better," she said in quite a strong voice when she had done. "Thank you."

He smiled at her and let his hand rest near hers in case she wished to take it.

"You will marry Alice," she said presently.

"I hope so, dear Auntie Belle."

"She'll have my money. I've some of my own. Even if her uncle has disowned her."

"It doesn't matter," said John. "I don't want Alice's money."

"But I want you to have it." She became very agitated and shifted about restlessly against the pillow. "I want to give you something."

"Thank you, dear Auntie Belle," said John, trying to soothe her. "I'd love to have anything that you'd like to give me and I'll take good care of it."

"Except Emily's letters," she said with a sudden little flash of her old malice.

"I messed that up," agreed John. "But they are all at the bottom of the River Cherwell now and not much use to anybody."

"And he's dead too. He was so sure I would die first and that no one would ever know."

"Ever know what?" prompted John. Surely there could not be still more revelations to come? And yet Lady Heron seemed to be making a tremendous effort, girding herself up to tell him something more.

"That I saw Emily die," she said at last, speaking very slowly and carefully, conserving her strength. "I was— striding on—ahead of the others. I was—very athletic— then."

"Yes, dear, yes," said John, fondling the withered hand.

"She was still breathing. And—she spoke to me."

"What did she say?" asked John, bending lower to catch the reply.

"She said—'Roddy did it. He hit me.'"

Lady Heron's labouring breaths reproduced only too vividly the last words of that other dying woman.

"Don't tell anyone," she whispered. "It doesn't matter now."

He gave his promise and she acknowledged it with a small movement of the hand.

"That's how it was," she said.

"I believe you, dearest Auntie Belle."

John thought she had done, but a little later she opened her eyes once more and motioned that she wanted to drink.

"Emily wanted . . ." she said when he had replaced the glass . . . "wanted me to . . ." She paused. "To punish him for her. But I didn't. Not till too late. Because I . . ."

Her mouth began to tremble and her whole face contorted itself into grotesque movements as she struggled to speak.

"Because I . . ."

The words were just audible and then the mouth stopped twisting and remained open, gasping, and the eyelids drooped for the last time.

"Because you loved him too," murmured John, getting to his feet and standing looking down at the bed with his hands clasped lightly together in front of him and his head bowed in the stance of an undertaker.

He stood there for a few minutes, motionless, with the great weight of dead passions, love and grief, hatred and anger and fear, pressing down upon his body and heart and mind. Then he took a deep breath, straightened up and shook himself, and called the nurse from the back room before going down to break the news to Alice.

Anna Clarke was born in Cape Town, and educated in Montreal and Oxford. She holds degrees in both Economics and English Literature, and has had a wide variety of jobs, mostly in publishing and university administration. She is the author of fourteen previous suspense novels, including *One of Us Must Die*, *Letter From the Dead*, and *Game Set and Danger*, published by the Crime Club.